2-

THE
KING'S EVIL

A NOVEL

WILL HEINRICH

Scribner

NEW YORK   LONDON   TORONTO   SYDNEY   SINGAPORE

SCRIBNER
1230 Avenue of the Americas
New York, NY 10020

SCRIBNER and design are trademarks of Macmillan Library Reference USA, Inc., used under license by Simon & Schuster, the publisher of this work.

For information about special discounts for bulk purchases, please contact Simon & Schuster Special Sales: 1-800-456-6798 or business@simonandschuster.com

Designed by Kyoko Watanabe
Text set in Aldine

Manufactured in the United States of America

1   3   5   7   9   10   8   6   4   2

Library of Congress Cataloging-in-Publication Data
Heinrich, Will.
The king's evil : a novel / Will Heinrich.
p.   cm.
I. Title.
PS3608.E38K56 2003
813'.6—dc21   2003042374

ISBN 0-7432-3504-5

But I say unto you, That ye resist not evil:
but whosoever shall smite thee on thy right cheek,
turn to him the other also.

MATTHEW 5:39

If he come to slay thee, forestall by slaying him.

SANHEDRIN 72A

THE
KING'S EVIL

CHAPTER ONE

1

I was thirteen when I stopped drawing. I became a painter instead. Not painting but simply being a painter, pure and bare, was enough for me and with little interruption lasted four years. But my idea could not survive forever in the world, and when I turned seventeen it occurred to me to enter a museum. I was the child of educated parents and the student of fine schools and I had, of course, been dragged through museums and museums, world without end; but I had never gone by free choice or entered, so to speak, with my eyes open. There was a retrospective of the Dutch artist Piet Mondrian at the Museum of Modern Art, and a reviewer, quoted in advertisements, had called him "too difficult for ordinary eyes." But I was a painter; I was seventeen.

I walked calmly through the first room, studying each picture in turn with respectful condescension. I saw a landscape with a ditch, a wood, a cow eating grass next to pointed hayricks. This man Mondrian, I thought, had a talent, but one that was safely muffled. The images were all without sharp definition, as were the colors, and it was not to any end that I could see. I would have said that he had found the street he wanted but not the house. I looked at my watch and realized that if Mondrian was no harder than this I would leave the show much too early for lunch.

I stopped in front of the hayricks feeling unhappy at the prospect of a slow and tedious morning and trying to make the best of it. I was, at the time, sufficiently flexible of mind that I found other things to look at. I was surprised to discover that the brown and white cow wore on her back only the suggestion of a pattern, but one that was of clear intent, one that mirrored the clouds in the sky. The grass was in its color really an ocean, the hayricks reflected the church steeple, there was a crescent moon in the dark blue sky. The line of trees and building tops that divided heaven from earth, the blue from the green, was a painting in itself—just in time I noticed the badly painted girl beside the cow. I had not noticed her yet because her blue dress did not stand out from the dark grass, because her perspective was flawed, and because she was perfectly flat. She was a blue smudge with vague yellow hair and only a gesture toward features: she was clearly a mistake. Thus reassured I congratulated the painter for the successes of his painting, and myself for my generosity of spirit.

I was further reassured, as I continued, by a self-portrait and a portrait of a girl with flowers. The hayricks had seemed to point to powerful colors, but he had lost his edge, and the brown colors of the painted artist were nothing better than adept. They hesitated. The girl and her flowers were even better: cheap, sentimental, and frightened of sharp lines. I mean to say that Mondrian set me up for an ambush, because I walked in the next room directly into sight of his *Windmill in Sunlight* and I swayed on my feet.

A glorious red windmill burst out against a yellow sky, at the bottom dissolving into its own reflection: a pond set in an orange ground, at the top leaning back proudly, its arms tall in unmoving majesty. The painting was made of thick lines of color, wavering or broken, that were all on the point of resolving into perfection.

At that age, if someone mentioned marriage or love, it did not bother me, because I had already kissed a girl and that was more or less the same thing. But if I saw with my own eyes two lovers walking down the road with arms entwined, I walked the other way; I could not pretend that this was not something different. What I could not dismiss I denied. But this windmill in sunlight entranced me: I could ignore it no more than I could comprehend it. I stood before the painting as if before God, experiencing transcendence but still feeling overwhelmed, until finally I took a few shaken steps to the next one.

I was subdued. The next few paintings were closer in style to the self-portrait, though better, but I was quiet; I felt nothing but the dull peace of convalescence. I had no relationship with these paintings, I passed them by with wary respect. I tried to save my strength because it was clear that they were leading to more beauty. A delicate white chrysanthemum, for example, I only glanced at. I stumbled my way with shame and humility to a tall red amaryllis, in a light blue bottle, in a blue field.

I saw this *Amaryllis* with some relief. It was more perfect than the windmill, but also more static, more subtle so more contained, more fully realized and therefore less dynamic. The painter had in his ascent trembled my earth and disturbed the air before my eyes, but with this flower he was safely away in heaven. There was as much intelligence, I thought, in this painting as in the other, but it did not shine out from the wall and demand my attention. I could admit to myself that it was a great painting and then leave it alone. But it was not yet so great that it was past all need to be looked at.

I stood and enjoyed the amaryllis; I forgot the time; I was glad to be there. When I finally began walking again, I dismissed the strangely colored landscapes that I passed as irrelevant. I ignored their evolution and decided that they represented an artist's vacation from his true progress. The ambush this time was more subtle—all I felt, when I came on *The Red Mill*, was mild surprise. I think that I even said to myself, That's rather large.

The painting was almost as tall as I was at the time, and its color and design were simple. There was a massive red windmill in a field of nocturnal blue; a brief, slightly darker blue divided ground from sky. If not for the windmill's moving arms, the picture would have been symmetrical, but such symmetry is meaningless; it would have been impossible, even by mathematical implication, to divide that great and solitary tower in two.

I could not walk away from it, and as I stood before it, it began to burn itself into my eyes and entirely into me. After a few seconds I heard a rushing sound as if my eyes and my ears and body were opening to the sheer force of the red mill, wider and wider. My use of the term "God" in describing the last windmill now seems trivial because this red windmill *was* God, great and terrible, and I cowered before it.

And then the presence was withdrawn and I continued. As I moved through room after room, I came to the conclusion that I had been measured by that mill and had failed. The experiments with black lines and gray colors ignored me, and then when the work readmitted pink and orange and blue, it did not need me at all. As the colors turned to squares and the squares to grids I felt that the meaning of this painting was moving further and further away from me.

I came to a great diamond of crossing gray lines. The square canvas had been turned over so that its corners pointed left and right and toward heaven and earth: it was an all-encompassing spiritual prison. And I came, finally, to the works for which Mondrian is best known, his irregular black and white grids with squares of primary color. It was now eleven in the morning; I stood before those perfect dangerous squares until the museum closed for the night. I spent the long day staring at paintings that shone to me bright and impenetrable as a beetle's shell: hostile, alien, opaque. They did not waver before my eyes, but I did not intend to leave until I had broken them open, and in the end I was gently led out by a uniformed guard.

I was so silent and withdrawn at dinner that evening that my mother began to cry. I was touched by this only insofar as I was briefly glad, after she had stormed out of the room, that my father did not speak to me. I sat in my dark bedroom for an hour or two after dinner, not quite thinking, and went to sleep, and in the morning I returned to the museum.

I walked quickly through the first rooms, excited to attempt the squares again, noticing with pleasure that everything I passed seemed small. I was almost running when I reached the room I wanted. I stopped abruptly before *Tableau I* and rubbed my eyes—it was the difference between twilight and noon. My body shook and I transcended myself entirely with a joy such as I had not known since early childhood. This artist had distilled painting to its very essence: with five colors and two lines he had achieved perfection. If his *Red Mill* was the God of Israel, mighty and terrible, his *Composition with Yellow Lines* was the God of Spinoza, abstract, incorruptible, eternal.

Again I spent the whole day in the museum, never eating, never sitting down, and the time seemed to pass in a moment. I was enraptured by a trinity of perfection: perfection of skill, perfection of understanding, and perfection of beauty. The day was a mighty day and I its conspirator. I believe it to be literally true that if someone had asked me my name then, I would not have known what to say, and would have felt, moreover, a great resentment for the impurity of language.

But in the late afternoon, I remembered myself for a moment, and I was a painter. This idea of myself as a painter, which for four years had been my foundation, now seemed wrong, but I did not know why. From the moment that I thought of this until I was again gently led out by a museum guard, I wandered through the exhibit's last few rooms, in search, as if I had forgotten the name of a favorite book, of something to remind me.

That evening at dinner I was not withdrawn but distracted, and I just managed to keep my corner of the conversation off the ground. This time in my room I flipped through a dozen books, unable to concentrate, because in addition to being preoccupied with my question I was nervous, ever increasingly nervous, that the question's solution would be terrible.

On the third morning I took my time eating breakfast and walked to the train station one careful step at a time. I knew that the answer would visit me suddenly with the first sight of a painting; I knew, in fact, that it was already with me but that only those five perfect colors and two perfect lines could force me to acknowledge it. I drew out the trip to the museum as much as I could, but I did not abandon it, and in the event, because I had slept badly and awoken early, I arrived as they opened the doors.

The early paintings hung quietly in the empty galleries and offered me courage. I walked directly through, feeling, so to speak, their hands on my shoulders as I passed. But when I came to *Tableau I,* I suffered no terrible epiphany. I felt only the same joy it had given me the day before, or at least a warm comfort in the memory of that joy. When nothing more happened I began to feel relief. This is to say that the ambush waited this time and came from behind—I felt the idea well up from my body into my head and then issue from my eyes to change the character of the painting before me. The perfect lines were not smiling, now: they gloated.

What this painter had accomplished was not the attainment of a moral perfection, or the depiction of a general aesthetic perfection: he had effected, more simply, the perfection of paint-

ing. He had distilled the art of painting into its purest essence
and rendered it complete. And every painting that had pointed
at God or the muse or money or fame now pointed at *Composition with Yellow Lines*. In *Composition with Yellow Lines*, therefore,
the progress came to rest. It was done.

This was my terrible epiphany: it was done. I would not be
a painter. I would not paint. This man Mondrian had stolen it
from me.

2

I realized in the museum show that I could not be a painter
because painting was finished. I saw that it would not matter if
all the paintings before me were destroyed and forgotten, or if I
worked in a distant forest and burned all of my own work as
soon as it was done. Human beings all move forward together;
no one can escape the draw of the rest, and no one moves alone.
As I dwelled on this fact it became worse and worse. Standing in
that museum I could not fail to see that if Mondrian had not
been born in Holland, he would not have painted his wind-
mills, and his monochromatic windmill with crossed arms was
the very parent, I believed, of his squares and lines. At the age of
seventeen I wanted to believe in the freedom of the individual,
but Mondrian had been nothing but a product of his time and
place, and so must we all be.

For a few terrible minutes I did not see how I could go on
living, or rather, why I should. But my problem was solved by
the same sincere naïveté that had created it. It occurred to me

that none of the people around me, who were all pursuing their own lives with apparent unconcern, could have realized what I had just realized about the nature of humanity. I was therefore unique, a sort of prophet of futility. Because I understood the true weight of fate, I alone was free, and I could look down from my cliff with an expression of elevated sorrow. I would have such compassion for my blind cousins that I would have no pity left for myself, and there were no worthwhile ends beyond this compassion to which I ever need exercise my freedom. This was perfect; being a painter threatened to require painting, but this new idea required nothing but itself.

I spent the rest of the day doing what I should have done in the first place, enjoying the art as art. But I did not walk out unaffected: like Jacob at Peniel I limped. I no longer expected to change the world or to make any mark on it. With my great work done, as I thought, in a brief flicker of understanding, I expected nothing more of myself than to hold a job and take care of a family if I should have one. I expected myself, in short, to be an unremarkable, unremarkably decent person, and this is what I did.

3

The hope and ambition of my youth fell whole without leaving a trace. I attended a university where I worked hard and without imagination and finished in the top of the class. I did not smoke or drink or play cards, I did not experiment with opiates or girls or religion. I had learned in the museum that I would be much happier on the whole if I simply pretended that art did not exist, and to be safe I condemned with it music, theater, literature, and conversation. I could be friends only with others as dull and sincere as I was but, because they did not have as grand a reason as I did for ignoring art, I could not help despising them. I trapped myself in the lowest possible form of human society, a web of inconclusive friendships not close or lasting enough to provide any true fellowship but just demanding enough to prevent me from learning to rely on myself.

After college I went to law school. I speculate sometimes that I chose law because I confused it with justice and justice with fate—I had frequent bad dreams about fate. But I do not know if I meant to escape pain by learning to understand it or escape it simply by helping to dispense it. Probably my entering law school represented nothing so much as a strategic retreat; I had wanted to be a lawyer when I was small because that is what my father was. He had been principal in a number of significant human rights cases and was very well known and very well thought of; by the time I was born, he had become the lawyer for several very large, very rich charitable foundations and was himself very large and very rich. When I graduated from law school he wrote me a letter of recommendation, and the following week I was employed, pending my examinations.

I made no secret of the fact that the details of the work did not matter as much to me as the mere fact of its accomplishment, so I quickly became the man that my genteel firm relied on to draw up wills, visit the infirm, and do whatever else was dull and unavoidable. Long beery dinners with patronizing colleagues replaced the awkward dry dinners of college. One by one I lost my dull and sincere college classmates, my few childhood friends, and my personal interests—I became a man with nothing to say. At the time, naturally, I did not see it this way; I considered myself to have grown into a responsible adult.

I think that if nothing had disturbed my progress, I might very well have faded slowly into nothingness. The year that I turned forty, for example, I noticed without much interest that I knew only two women, the secretary of my firm and my mother. I rarely said more than hello to either of them. My course was disturbed, however, by my father's illness. I tried to prevent my mother's hysterical nursing, but I could not: no argument about her risk of infection or his need for rest could compel her to drop his hand or leave his side, and so finally they lay dying together and I was left alone.

I could not bear to listen to their hoarse whispering in the evenings as they reminisced about their wedding or my father's early career, or even to be in the same house with it, and so I began visiting the library every day to read about their killer. I quickly developed an abstract appreciation for the study of tuberculosis, an appreciation that grew stronger every day even as it moved further from my parents and the real effects of the disease. It was the first time in decades that I had felt a sincere interest in anything, the first time that I was not painfully, tediously aware of the ticking of my watch. As my parents' death grew closer, my interest in their disease grew into a passion, and it became something like an avocation to me, the thing that made me human.

They died within minutes of each other, and within hours I found myself in an office in my own law firm, nodding gravely as I listened to their wills. I had no time to react. I signed where I was directed to sign and suddenly found myself rich.

My father left me an astonishing amount of money, so much that if it had occurred to me to think about it I would not have been able to imagine its being legitimately come by. But it did not occur to me to think about it (or indeed about their deaths or my loss) because I was immediately terrified by the much greater problem of what to do with it.

For years I had lived my life on the premise that responsible adults work responsibly; but I could not fool myself that my job was really of use to anyone, and I now had more than enough money to live on for the rest of my life. I wanted to give the money away and forget about it, but to do so for the sake of a pointless job would only serve to emphasize its pointlessness. Moreover the limits of my father's charity had been very strictly defined, and I half believed that he would come back to haunt me if I gave all his money away. To go to work every morning while the money sat in the bank would be ridiculous, but I had no idea what I might do with myself except go to work every morning. I did not know what to do.

For weeks I put off thinking about the problem while growing more and more nervous. I stopped reading and slept badly. One night I lay awake almost until dawn and then in the morning I overslept. The streets were nearly empty when I walked to my office in the late morning and I felt comforted by the quiet, less nervous than I had been in days. I took enough pleasure in the walk that I tried to prolong it by walking slowly, and I began to look at and notice the street before me, the buildings beside me, the sky above me.

As I finally, reluctantly, approached my firm's building, I noticed a small crack down in the building's wall. Out of the crack grew a small orange flower. I do not know what sort of flower it was and indeed it might have been a weed. But it was small and light and, to me, beautiful. I stooped down to look at it and forgot the time. When I stood up I remained transfixed and did not move. I wondered how many times before I had passed this orange blossom without noticing it. It could not have been very many since it was early spring and the flower was young; nevertheless, even once seemed too much, so I turned away from my office door and walked home.

No one was surprised when I gave my resignation. I saw some of them, once or twice, on the street, and they looked the other way to avoid the trouble of saying hello. It did not bother me. My sky had been overcast for twenty years and for the first time I saw light.

Looking at the date of my last paycheck and the date on the purchase deed of the house that I went on to buy, I can determine that I spent about six weeks walking through the city noticing small orange flowers in the cracks in the walls. At the time it seemed to be a lifetime, and even now, with the dates before me, I would maintain that it was. Those weeks certainly contained more life than the years that went before them. I did not miss company or love because the simple sensual world was overwhelming me with its beauty and wonder—the very air was so intoxicating to me that I sometimes forgot to move. I would awake suddenly every morning, not because of anxiety now but from eager excitement, and hurry into my clothes. I would have bread and water for breakfast because anything more complicated would be too much to assimilate: the taste and texture of cold water in a glass was of infinite depth. Then, sometimes after stopping dead in the middle of my floor to stare at the sunlight sloping in through the window, I would hurry out the door. The whole day I spent walking through the city, its streets and parks, learning how to hear, how to see, and how to be.

I also learned, as a child does, to discriminate. The day after I resigned my job, the second day of my new life, was more wonderful than my second day in the museum, and the dirty corner of a sidewalk more perfect than the painter's yellow lines. But discrimination is also a pleasure, and I began gradually to find some things more beautiful than others. I found, for example, that I enjoyed walking on the street better when I knew that I was walking to the park, and I found that I enjoyed being in the park better in the early morning of a working day when no one else was there.

If some things are more beautiful, of course, then some things must be ugly, and I began to see this, too. At first even this was a pleasure: I would stand rooted to the ground in front of a gaudy billboard, thinking it terribly ugly and thrilled at the strength of my feeling. But once I began having this sort of feeling, I had it often and its pleasure did not last long. The city is full of ugly billboards, ugly noises, and ugly people.

At the time I was still trying to be a good person, and what this meant to me then was living for others at my own expense. Clearly I did not succor the poor or comfort the dying, and I did not give away any of my father's legacy. These would have been excessive. But in every small human interaction, in every way possible in the course of my normal life, I bent myself back for someone else's comfort. In argument I was always wrong, in waiting rooms I was always last, and I was always in the way. So while now I might feel inclined, having had my foot stepped on by some arrogant young banker, to step on his foot in turn, then I merely stayed out of his way. I hid in the parks and the book-stores, where the bankers and ugly billboards could not reach me, and eventually I left.

I do not remember how I first heard of Bettley. It is an unre-markable town in the far north, unlikely to come up in urban conversation. But I knew the name for some reason, and one day, hiding in a bookstore from the ugly street, I picked up an atlas and found it on a map. The next day, having nothing else to do, I bought a train ticket and rode up. It was the first trip I had taken anywhere since my childhood, and it was far better than any family vacation. For the first time in my life I considered the possibility that my great city was not the center of the earth, or at least not an all-encompassing center. The trees astonished me and so did the train platforms. It was a slow country train and I could have stepped out and looked at any of the towns we traveled through, but it was enough for me to stay in my seat and look out.

I think that I would have been happy to ride the train to the northernmost ice, but my ticket said Bettley, so there I got off. There is no hotel or restaurant in Bettley, no plaza or arcade, so after leaving the station I walked through the town. There was one main road through the middle and a small complex of narrow alleys at the town's proudest center. The store was closed for a local holiday.

The main road continued out of the town again and seemed to disappear into a forest of fir trees, and I followed it without a thought. In my first act of imagination since Mondrian, I saw the tall firs as mighty wooded statesmen, and I entered as a humble visitor to their sylvan parliament. The road bent to the left, and once the town was definitely gone it bent right again, and in the elbow was my house, a strange blocky structure painted bluish green. It seemed more like the realization of a schematic diagram than it did like any other house I had ever seen.

I knocked on the door and was invited in to tea. The widower who lived there explained that he had dreamed the house as a young man but gone on to marry a wife who refused to see it built. (In fairness to his wife I will say that the house did look as if it had been planned out with toy blocks, and it was painted a strange and threatening color.) When he had, against expectation, outlived his wife, and done so with money in the bank, he decided that his task was to build the house he had once dreamed. He hired local carpenters who were too happy to have work to come to any judgment about the design, and they built it. He also decided that, old widower though he was, he wanted fresh milk for his breakfast, and he had cut down enough trees across the road to plant grass for a cow and build her a shed to live in. But with all this done he had recently begun to feel tired and cold and was thinking of moving south.

Both of us having plenty of money it took no more than a

friendly minute or two to arrive at the figure that I wrote on my check. As a seal to the contract he offered to take me across the road to see the cow and give me some milk for my tea. She was a sweet-tempered brown cow with a white cloud pattern across her back. She took to me immediately, and this was enough for the old man: he invited me to move in right away and stay with him in the blue-green house until his own travel arrangements were made. That evening we took a walk together and I met some of my new neighbors. The next day when I returned to the city to pack up my belongings it already felt foreign to me; after throwing some books and clothing in a trunk I hurried back north resolved to conduct any further business by mail. The widower's arrangements did not take long and soon he was gone.

For twenty years and more I had done my duty to be good in the driest possible way, unmotivated by any real human sentiment, but now I found that to smile as I passed a woman on Bettley's main street, or to hold open the door of the store as a man walked out with packages, gave me boundless pleasure. I was happy and grateful all the time and I needed nothing else. In the eternal mornings I walked in the quiet forest and in the afternoons I read by an open window with the pine smell in my mouth. Sometimes I played cards at the store. And if, on my way down the road, I had the chance to raise my hat to some shy little girl, I considered my day well spent.

This happiness of mine reached its apex when I was able to give a drink of fresh milk to a small boy passing through town with his mother. I had found them at the train station waiting for a connection, so I took them home with me and gave them lunch. I brought the little boy out with me to milk the cow, and I gave him a glass, and he thanked me so sweetly that I was sorry to see him go. I stood on the platform and waved to him until his train was out of sight.

I lived this way for years.

CHAPTER TWO

Abel came into Bettley with rain. He probably arrived at the station, having stowed away or stolen money for a ticket, but it is possible that he walked. It would have taken him several hours to walk from the closest town. When he got here he had thirty dollars in his pocket, a clasp knife, and a gold pen with the initials LMS. He might have gone into a hotel if there were one, or a restaurant, but the store had closed at eight o'clock and the town street was empty.

It would not have taken the boy long to find the store, and once he had found it I do not think it took him any time at all to break the lock. We have only one store in the town, so nearly anything a person might need is kept in it somewhere. Abel found dry clothing to change into and hid his own wet clothes in the storeroom. He ate some bread and drank a small bottle of wine. When I saw the shopkeeper the next day, he told me that Abel had left a crust of bread and the wine bottle next to the cash register. He had also opened the cash register and taken out a ten-dollar bill, which he left on the counter under the bottle. There is a small jewelry counter in the store that he did not touch. All things considered, it might have seemed an understandable and forgivable forced entry if the shopkeeper had not known how much money should have been in the cash drawer, and if Abel had not stopped to urinate against the inside of the door. (I did not think of it at the time, but this is a particularly disquieting act because the shop has no back door: he must have walked through his own mess to get out.)

Taking no umbrella or jacket with him he left the store and began walking again. I do not know where he intended to go, but then I do not know where he came from. I imagine that he had been driven out of his last home and was wandering aimlessly. I do know that my house is not visible from in town, so he must either have left the town with the intention of walking on or have set out especially to look for a more isolated house.

There are many reasons why he might have done this latter, some mundane and some frightening, but the simplest possible reason is that houses in Bettley have porches. Every house and building in town has a short front porch, and the boards these porches are made of are invariably old. I can imagine Abel stepping onto one old porch, hearing the creak it made, and deciding to look for a house without one.

Probably the best answer is that he walked out of town with the intention of walking all night but the storm got worse as he passed my house. I lived alone and I had not made my house look lived in; indeed, except for the study and the kitchen, it was not. At night, to a tramp, it may look abandoned.

The front door is metal, flush with the wall, and has no doorknob, only a keyhole. The back door is the same, but it is inside an enclosed porch with a screen door that does not lock. The old widower had, in fact, had tramps in mind; once one had gotten into his former house and fallen asleep in his bed. "I don't mind giving a bed to a traveling man," he told me, "but not my bed." So he made sure that the doors would be hard to get past, and that the windows were high off the ground, but he built a cushioned bench into the back porch so that anyone who took the trouble to look would find a place to get out of the rain.

It was only much later that I happened to look at my doors carefully and saw the scrapes around the keyholes. I presume that Abel made them with his knife. It does not seem to be a credit to his intelligence that he tried to get in the back door after failing on the front door, since their locks are identical, but I imagine that he was only frustrated. I can see him, his dark hair wet, his shirt not warm enough, filled with hatred for whoever designed the house's doors. It must have seemed clearly abandoned, waiting to shelter him, but he could not get in.

He would have gone around to the back, and his hopes were probably raised for a moment by the screen door, and then toppled again by the same terrible lock. He tried again. Finally he stretched out on the cushioned bench as well as he could, his arms close to his body for warmth as he listened to the storm. The wind woke me up several times that night, but if Abel had been walking all day he would not have had trouble falling asleep.

CHAPTER THREE

1

I was in the habit of spending the first day of every month in springtime and early fall in the pine forests. There being no church in Bettley and the pines, I will admit now, always striking more reverence into my soul than the crucifixion, these days served as a sort of religious observance. I would pack up bread and cheese and a bottle of water, along with a notebook, a novel, and a pen, and spend the day silently wandering. I would always come home with a sore neck from looking up through branches to the sky. I do not believe that I ever opened either the novel or the notebook, although I sometimes went as far as taking the pen in my hand.

Sometimes I also brought Diana Greene. Passing her on her porch one morning I had awkwardly invited her to come with me; she did, and for a few minutes we walked in shy silence.

Finally I cleared my throat and told her about imagining the trees as a parliament; she answered me at once that she always thought of them as cities, peopled by insects and birds. After that I saw her often, but I did not always invite her on my walks because our conversation left no attention for the trees.

On the morning of the first of June I awoke when it was still dark. The time before dawn, or the dawning itself, always reminded me of my father's brother. I would stay with him sometimes when my parents traveled. He used to play a game with me: if he found me taking something in the kitchen, for example, or standing on the couch in my shoes to reach a book, he would make a grim expression. "What are you doing?" he would demand. I always froze, confident in my uncle's good intentions but physically intimidated by his size and his presence. As he stood and stared at me and I trembled and stared back, his face would slowly soften. So slowly that the change was imperceptible, the corners of his mouth would turn up. Finally he was smiling, and then grinning, and he would dance over to where I was laughing but still rooted to my spot and lift me up to stand on the back of the couch, or cry out, "There are better cookies on the other shelf!" Sometimes, too, he would creep into the room where I was reading, and I would catch the movement in the corner of my eye but pretend that I had not seen him; he would move toward me in a slow crouch. Then he would begin saying, "Bump, bump, bump," as his feet touched the floor, louder and louder, until he grabbed me and whirled me, laughing hysterically, around the room.

I made myself tea and toast and sat looking out the kitchen window at the friendly shade of my uncle, pink creeping dawn.

When I could more or less see the ground, and could distinguish the trees from one another, I put my plate in the sink, picked up my bag, and walked out the back door. I was on the porch and had already closed and locked the door before I saw the boy lying on the bench.

I had never seen a dead body, and I did not think that this was one, but he did not seem to be merely sleeping. He lay flat on his back with his arms straight down his body, his mouth slightly open, and his eyes closed, and I could not tell if he was breathing. I was also, after a moment, unsettled by my own lack of initial reaction to finding him. I mean to say that I lived alone in a very small town in the far north, and it was the early morning, and I should have been frightened or at least startled to suddenly find a stranger on my porch. But I had not been, and in fact even after thinking of it I was not. I could not imagine this person that I had only just seen for the first time being anywhere else; I think without realizing it I considered him to have sprung fully formed from the couch he slept on. Then when I saw his eyelids flutter and his lower lip tremble under breath I felt enormous relief.

I leaned over to make sure of his breathing and took out my watch to let him fog its steel lid. It occurs to me now that this may have been the first time in my life that I really looked at someone sleeping; that may have been why he did not seem to me to be asleep. Because I had dreams of violent motion and color, I had always conceived of sleep as being dynamic, but this sleeping boy was frozen.

Not wanting to wake him I stood in the porch's far corner to examine him. He had dark wavy hair, a little long, but caught out of the way behind his head. He had deeply set eyes and the eyelids were dark. His coloring on the whole was confusing; he was white, even wan, but he somehow gave the impression that he should have been darker. He looked like someone from a sunny country who has been ill and indoors for several months. I could see that his lips were strong and thick.

In fact I did react to finding him: under surprise and stress, which I did not feel but which were there, time bent. I forgot about waking up that morning and about breakfast, and I forgot entirely about the waiting pine trees and waiting Diana. I was fascinated by the young face beneath me; I was almost as entranced as he was.

I tried for a few seconds to determine his age, but quickly gave it up. His face was old and his body young. I inspected his clothes: he wore a large, badly fitting white shirt and shapeless dark pants. These were new, but his shoes were rotting on his feet. His body on the whole was small and bony, although I could see that there was flesh to his arms. I think that his head must have been disproportionately large, or his body stunted, but even in his deathly sleep he had such charisma that I only just noticed it. Eventually I would decide with the doctor that he could not have been older than seventeen, and may have been as young as thirteen.

As he slept my eye was caught by something under his collar. I crept slowly across the wooden floor, afraid of making noise, until I stood almost by his head. I squatted down to look into the overlarge collar and see the bruises across his chest. There was only enough unbruised skin to make clear, by contrast, how badly beaten he must have been. The bruises all stopped at his neck except one greenish brown patch beneath his left ear. I stood and returned to the corner.

It seemed impossible that his bruises could have come from a fair fight; to be so thoroughly covered he would have had to have been carefully beaten by someone much bigger, perhaps while another person held him down. But he did not look at all beaten in spirit: he lay back on his couch like a sleeping king or like a stone Crusader on the lid of a sarcophagus. I was mystified and humbled by the boy's casual bravery.

I had heard parents describe "falling in love" with their children and always found it a very distasteful expression. I would have said that it was hyperbolic and extremely inappropriate; but I simply did not understand it. I did not have children of my own, and my own parents did not love me so much as the idea of their son, an office that I only happened to fill. But when my eyes fell on this sleeping boy's rotted shoes I felt pierced to the heart; I turned my eyes away, but the images stuck to me, his shoes, his bruises, his peaceful face—I fell in love.

Until now I had been anxiously asking myself, even as I examined him, what my responsibility would be. I liked my peaceful and unchanging life in Bettley, and I was unhappy at the thought of even a temporary disruption. I had wished for him to wake up because I did not want to wake him myself but wanted the whole thing settled quickly. But now I simply stood in the corner trying to contain myself while wishing for his sleep to be peaceful.

I do not know how long I stood there looking at him and waiting, but it cannot have been very long. The sky was still twilight when he opened his eyes. He looked around the porch first without moving, and then he turned his head. Keeping his gaze on me he sat up and turned toward me.

"Good morning," I said. I wanted to cry out, Trust me, I will not hurt you.

He looked me over carefully before answering.

"Is this your house?" he asked. His voice was clearly in its early adolescence, but he pronounced the words with care and confidence. I imagined that his shifting eyes indicated fear—although he was actually nothing more than careful—and I took no offense at the abruptness of his question.

"This is my house," I said. "My name is Joseph."

His eyes bore on me with surprising concentration and complete opacity.

"Joseph S. Malderoyce," I said. I cleared my throat. "What is your name?"

"My name is Abel Rufous," he said. He had begun looking around the porch again even as he answered; his eyes fell finally on the lock in the door. It will sound odd, but I felt that I was disturbing him; I felt impolite and intrusive for addressing him.

"It's only dawn," I said. "Why don't you come in?"

He nodded and stood up. I hurriedly unlocked the door and went up the stairs, Abel following, to the guest room. I was excited; he was only the second person I had ever had in, and I knew that Diana, the first, did not like the green house any more than its first owner's wife had. He followed me silently into the guest room and sat down on the bed. I realized that he must have been half asleep still and I forgave him his silence.

"Why don't you go back to sleep for a couple of hours,

Abel?" I said. He nodded again and lay back on the bed, on top of the covers.

"Make yourself at home," I said, and I almost choked when I added, "take off your shoes." He only shook his head at this before his eyes fell closed again. I brought in a blanket, which I laid carefully over his body. He must have felt safer now, because he curled up on his side, one hand under his head and one between his knees. I closed the door softly.

For a moment outside the door I was overwhelmed by a strange fantasy. I wanted to pull the boy out of bed, drag or throw him down the wooden stairs, and lock him out of the house. . . . I horrified myself. I actually fell back against the wall, my knees weak, as I tried to discover the source of such an idea. Then I realized: it was my attachment to monotony. I did not resent Abel for appearing on my doorstep—far from it! My violent fantasy was only the fierce attempt of my animal sense of comfort to obstruct any change to my routine. I laughed with pleasure at this realization, as I thought it was, and happily discarded the fantasy. I had to go tell Diana that we could not take our planned walk and go bring the doctor.

2

I had not, since moving to Bettley, ever had occasion to call on the doctor. I had been introduced to him somewhere—probably in the store in winter, when people lingered by the stove—and although we did little more than shake hands I felt an instant sympathy with him. He was fairly tall and muscularly built, and would have been an imposing presence (particularly, this being the far north, in light of his dark black skin) had he not treated his own physical presence so lightly. Meeting him I felt as I had once felt as a child, sitting next to another boy I did not know in a new class. Books were being passed out, and this boy, being closer, took two and handed me one without thought, and I took it without thought, because we were already friends without speaking.

This morning in June I found the doctor sitting on his porch in town smoking a pipe. Before I could speak he saw the expression on my face; he ducked inside to put down his pipe and book, locked the door, and followed me home. It was not until we reached my door and I hesitated that it occurred to me to explain.

"I found a boy asleep on my porch this morning," I said as I opened the door. "I brought him in and put him to bed, but his shirt was too big and I could see through his collar that he was bruised all over his chest. He didn't undress, so I don't know if there's anything else. . . ."

"That's enough," the doctor answered. Just then I thought of Diana, and I stood nervously looking back and forth between the stairs and the front door. Dr. Ericsson raised his eyebrows inquisitively.

"Oh," I said, "I just remembered that I was supposed to see Diana Greene this morning."

"I'll be fine alone with the boy," he answered, "but you should come in with me, first, so I don't scare him."

I led the doctor up the stairs to the guest room and knocked on the door. Abel did not answer. I knocked again.

"Is he sleeping?" the doctor asked.

"I think so," I said, and opened the door. We found Abel sitting up on the bed looking toward us as we came in. He did not look entirely present. I do not mean that his mind was somewhere else, because he was staring at us and around the room with great concentration; but he seemed as if he were sitting in the middle of a play trying to figure out what was going on, essentially distant from all the players. I found him intimidating.

"Good morning again," I said, trying to smile. "This is Abel." Abel looked at the doctor, who had put one hand on my shoulder.

"I'm Dr. Ericsson," he said. "Joe brought me over to take a look at you."

"Why?"

"Because he could see the bruises under your collar," the doctor answered. He turned to me and told me I could go.

I went into town to Diana's house to tell her that I could not see her. For some reason I was unwilling to explain the circumstances but equally unwilling simply to end our conversation; finally she shut the door impatiently and I went home. At the time the doctor told me only his conclusions, but much later he told me the details of what had happened while I was gone:

Once I had closed the door, and my footsteps had become quiet, Abel looked the doctor in the eye.

"I've never heard of a nigger doctor before," he said. Dr. Ericsson, being the only black person for quite some distance apart from his wife, had of necessity learned to ignore casual insensitivities, but this was hardly a casual insensitivity. The boy seemed to be trying to bait him, and the doctor looked down at his somewhat stunted body from his own six feet and smiled at his confidence.

"Will you undress, please?" he said. Abel turned his face away, so the doctor approached the side of his bed and began unbuttoning his shirt. When Abel tried to shake him off, the doctor pressed him back into the bed, turning him so that his legs came onto the bed as well. Held down, Abel could not reach with his arms so he kicked the doctor in the shoulder; the doctor stopped the undressing for a moment and dropped one heavy fist into Abel's thigh.

Abel did not let his own crying distract him and managed to bite the doctor's hand as he was starting for the shirt buttons again. The doctor pressed his fist into the boy's open mouth while he finished getting the shirt off. Abel's chest was black with bruises.

"Will you tell me what happened?" he asked. As he said this he touched the bruises lightly with his fingers. Abel did not answer. After the boy threw the doctor's hands off again, the doctor leaned over to speak directly into his ear. "Listen to me, little boy," he whispered. "I'm bigger than you are and no one will notice a few extra bruises. Do you understand?"

Abel turned his face away, and Dr. Ericsson reached out and turned it back. "I asked you if you understood," he said.

"I understand." Abel shut his eyes and submitted to the examination. Dr. Ericsson, seeing no gross fractures of the ribs, asked him whether he had been beaten elsewhere on his body and began conducting a general exam. He listened to the boy's heart, looked into his ears and eyes and down his throat, had him stand on one leg, checked his strength and reflexes.

"All right," the doctor said, "you can get dressed."

Abel sullenly put his shirt back on. The doctor sat down in the chair by the door.

"Tell me something, Abel," he said. "What is two plus two?"

"Seventy-five," he answered.

"What about the square root of one hundred and forty-four?"

"Oh," Abel said, "that's a tough one."

"Is it?" Dr. Ericsson found a tennis ball under his seat that just missed Abel's head.

"Twelve," Abel muttered. He lay down on the bed and turned away from the doctor.

"What's the opposite of wood?"

"Dew," Abel said, and the doctor laughed. He laughed because he was pleased with Abel's answer, but Abel turned over and threw the tennis ball at him.

"You will realize," the doctor said, having caught the ball and thrown it back, "that you give me no special reason to treat you with courtesy. In fact you've given me a special motive to be discourteous. Would you like to try again? I suggest that you politely tell me your name and ask after my health."

Abel was already lying down with his back to the doctor, but now he moved and turned ostentatiously as if to face still more away. The doctor stood up and opened the door. He spoke more gently now. "I only laughed at your answer because it surprised me," he said. "I didn't hope for a better answer than metal. Yours was very intelligent."

Abel turned over and stared up at Dr. Ericsson with hateful eyes.

"You flatter me, *doctor*," he said. The doctor laughed again and closed the door.

After returning from Diana's I had sat down in my study and nervously tried to read. I hoped that the boy was not too badly hurt, or at least I thought I did. I realize now that that same urge toward monotony that had pictured my throwing the boy down the stairs was busy praying that he would have some serious medical problem that would take him out of town south to the hospital. When the doctor knocked, I leaped up out of my chair to open the door.

"Come in," I said. "Please, how is he?"

The doctor looked around my study, smiling when he noticed my medical books, before he sat down.

"Biology?" he asked.

"An amateur interest in mycobacteria," I said. "What about Abel?"

"He seems very intelligent," the doctor said. "His emotional development is a different question."

"What about the bruises?"

"He wouldn't tell me anything," the doctor answered. "They're not so serious. Nothing is broken and they should all be gone in a few weeks."

"And is he healthy?"

"It's an interesting question," he said. "I don't think I could pin down anything specific that's wrong with him, apart from the fact that he's certainly been beaten up before. There's nothing really worth worrying about at the moment. Do you know anything about him but his name?"

"No."

"Not where he came from?"

"No."

The doctor raised an eyebrow. "Do you intend to keep him here?"

"What else can I do?" I asked, and I imagine that it sounded more like a plaintive demand than a rhetorical question. "I can hardly turn him out into the forest, and it would be almost as bad to bundle him onto the train and send him right to the nearest orphanage."

The doctor looked at his fingernails.

"It's your decision," he said. "He isn't very friendly, Joe."

I was so relieved that the doctor also found him unfriendly that I reacted with sympathy for the boy and proposed a fair-minded apology.

"No," I said, "but God knows what he's just come from."

"That's true."

"Was he very difficult with you?"

Dr. Ericsson looked at me carefully before answering.

"I didn't have any real trouble," he said, and that was as much as I heard about Abel's mouth and teeth for months. The doctor stood up and walked to my bookcase. He stood close and turned his head sideways to read the titles.

"You have a great collection," he said. "I almost wish there were an epidemic here so I could visit and do research."

He pointed at one large reference work. "May I?"

"Please," I said.

3

In the course of our subsequent conversation, the doctor asked me to call him Michael. He impressed me very much with his quick verbal intelligence, and I believe that I impressed him as well with my unlikely specialized knowledge. A conversation about disease developed into a conversation about life, and only when he remembered another patient that he was supposed to check on and looked at his watch did we realize how long we had been talking. He hastily handed back the book in his hand.

"I have to go look at my pregnancy," he said, "but thank you, Joe."

"It was a pleasure to talk to you," I said.

He shook my hand. "The pleasure was mine. I'll see you soon, I hope."

He began to turn away before he spoke again. "Do you mind if I make one suggestion?" he asked.

"Please," I said.

"You may have to teach him courtesy slowly."

"I don't doubt it."

"Don't be too friendly," he said. "I'll see you, Joe."

For the first week, at least, the doctor's warning did not seem to apply. I had gathered from what he said that he was afraid Abel would take advantage of kindness, but for the time he did not. He spent most of the first day in the guest room. I offered to show him around the house or the town, I invited him to come with me to milk the cow, but I did not press him when he did not respond. I brought him downstairs to eat lunch and then again to eat dinner. We hardly exchanged a word.

In fact we hardly spoke through that whole first week. We had achieved immediately what I would call the converse of my instant sympathy with Dr. Ericsson. I mean to say that Dr. Ericsson and I understood each other so well and so quickly that we had no need to test each other with small talk. In Abel's case, we did not even get as far as small talk—I did not because he was so mysterious to me, and he did not, I thought, because of his extreme caution. I was nervous and shy at having a guest live in my house, and I assumed that the guest would be at least as nervous and shy as I was. He may have been nervous; but he may also have been simply making sure of his impression of me before wasting his time talking.

He was helpful in an offhand manner. If I had put the kettle on and came in when it was whistling to turn it off, and he was sitting there, he would hand me my cup. He always put his dishes in the sink at the end of a meal. He did not offer to help wash them, but he was a child and a guest and I did not even think about it. Perhaps it was not because he was a child and a guest—more probably it was because I had lived alone for far too long and I seldom imagined any change in my routine so great as someone else washing dishes.

I gave him a book or two to read, a history and a novel, and he took short walks in town. Somehow the days passed, as they always did for me in Bettley, without much being done. But if the days passed quickly, the week was slow. By the time Abel had lived with me for a week I felt as if he had been there forever. I certainly felt that it was too late to demand to know where he had come from or to send him away. We had not spoken ten words to each other and he might have been my son.

I, at least, had gotten used to Abel and begun to take his presence for granted. I liked seeing another human being's face in the living room when I came in the door. I liked cooking for two people. I liked that we did not need to speak. His silent presence was, in fact, the perfect introduction to a longtime bachelor to no longer living alone.

Moreover, I do not say that he might have been my son merely to emphasize how thoroughly I had become accustomed to his presence. I mean also that I began to take for granted that that presence would continue. I took it for granted that he would live with me. I imagine this must seem strange, and I want to explain what I think are the three reasons that I came to feel this way. I will start with the reason that puts me in the worst light.

When the boy first arrived, I had a fantasy of throwing him down the wooden steps and locking him out of the house. I explained this to myself at the time as the reaction of my own spiritual inertia against an agent of change, and I still think that this explanation has some truth to it. By the time the boy had been there for a week, I had accepted his presence, and I think that the same part of me that at first imagined throwing the boy out now felt this: Now that he is here, for God's sake let that be the end of it. Once having gotten used to cracking open four eggs in the morning, I mean, I did not want to return to two.

The second reason, which morally at least is neutral, was loneliness. I have said that I was happy in Bettley and it is true, but it should be borne in mind that I had long since resigned myself to a life alone. It is not impossible to be happy when you have ceased to wish for more than you have, but once another person enters your home, even such a dark and silent boy, your former loneliness will take on a new and unattractive color.

Finally, I do not know why Abel picked my porch to sleep on, though I am certain that it cannot have had anything to do with me, but for whatever reason, he had. He had slept on the porch with such assurance, he had lived in my house for only a week with such gravity, that I felt he belonged here. I admit that the morally responsible course would have been to interrogate him aggressively about where he had come from and then either return him there or take the long train ride to an orphanage in the city. But even after a week this idea struck me not as a return but as an expulsion, and being more sentimental than I was moral, I simply did not have the stomach for it. I admit that I did not do what would have been best for him.

By the end of the week, Abel had begun talking a little, and I discovered that he was as intelligent as the doctor had suggested. I found him one morning in my study reading the *Dictionary of Mycobacteriology*. He was sitting at my desk leaning over the book, his face only an inch or two from the page, his lips moving as if he were whispering to it. He did not look up until I stood over his shoulder and spoke to him.

"I guess you find it interesting," I said.

"Are you a biologist?" he asked.

"I was a lawyer," I answered. I did not say more because already I was changing my behavior to follow Abel's: several days of his silent presence had left me silent as well, and only two or three days of his direct conversation left me speaking with the same shortness. Abel looked down at the book again.

"What is your interest in mycobacteria?"

I remember being impressed at how casually he pronounced this word.

"It's a hobby," I said. Abel looked across the room at the shelves full of studies and case histories, the albums of slides, and the microscope on the top shelf.

"Did you have a friend with tuberculosis?" he asked.

"More than one," I said. "I began reading about it after the first one died." I walked over to look at the books myself. I took down a small book about tuberculosis in India and began flipping the pages.

"That's only why I started reading, though," I said. "I very quickly stopped thinking of disease as involving real people."

"You must find it comforting to be an expert," Abel said. He pushed his dark hair away from his dark eyes.

"I'm not sure what you mean," I said.

"I mean that it's a small world where you know who you are and who everyone else is," he said. "Knowing about something gives you power over it."

"I see." I thought he was very perceptive.

"Also," he said, "I don't know if it's true of you, but in general, I think people like to have a way of being superior to other people. So you could tell yourself that it doesn't matter what I say, since I don't know about tuberculosis, or Russian history, or Romantic painting, which is what's really important."

I felt caught out and I laughed. "I don't know why that wouldn't be true of me, Abel," I said.

"You don't have very many law books."

"That's true," I said, and I was flattered that he remembered I had been a lawyer even though I had only mentioned it a moment before. I was always surprised when someone I knew demonstrated knowledge of anything about me that was not immediately and directly apparent. "But I didn't really like the law."

"May I guess again?" he asked. I did not know what he wanted to guess.

"Of course," I said.

"Your father was a lawyer."

"That's right." I laughed. He put down the book. "How are you so perceptive?"

Abel shrugged his shoulders. I sat down on the free chair, ready to ask Abel another question, but before I could he began asking me technical questions about what he had read. I became totally absorbed in a discussion about the essential nature of disease, and only when the boy stood up to wash his hands did I remember how old he was.

With the successful prosecution of this conversation, Abel decided to trust me. So I thought at the time; now I might be more inclined to say that, once having tested me on a specialized subject, he decided that it was more or less worth his time to talk to me. In either case, our new rapport led gradually to the heroic month of July.

CHAPTER FOUR

1

By the beginning of July I had come to love having Abel in my house. I had not forgotten that he was a runaway child, or that I did not know where he came from or who might be looking for him; on the contrary, I remembered this very well. But whenever the memory arose, I pushed it away and refused to think of it. In the same way, while I was not insensible of warning signs, I simply overlooked them. I did not want him to leave.

I had lived by myself for decades, and it is not surprising that after an initial acclimatization another soul in my house should make me happy. But Abel was more than this: he was an entire family in himself. I would wake him up in the morning and make him breakfast, and in that way I felt like his mother or father. I would have long discussions with him in the evenings on the porch, telling him about my childhood, confiding in him my long loneliness, and in that way he was like a brother to me. He was also, in practice, the first close friend that I had as an adult, since his age made me much less guarded around him than I was at that time around Michael and Diana. And I promise you I was so overjoyed at his sympathetic understanding that I never once paused at the vagueness of his replies, and never once felt awkward unburdening myself to a child.

I showed him around the town and took him for walks, and in that way he was like a visiting cousin. The English language suffers from the lack of an antonym for *loneliness;* I will propose not seriously but just for the moment the word *tribeliness.* I felt as I walked with Abel a *tribeliness* that was new and exhilarating, and I say he was like a cousin then because I felt that atavistic sort of double *tribeliness* that one gets from a sympathetic blood relative. I even began asking him for advice about this or that small matter, and in that way he was like an uncle to me or even a father.

One incident of his serving as a child I will describe in more detail. On the morning of the first day of July, at breakfast, Abel asked if he could tell me something.

"Anything," I said.

"When I came to Bettley," he said, and a thrill of excitement ran through me, "it was raining."

"I remember."

"My clothes were wet and I didn't have any others, and I—so I broke into the store in town. I stole the clothes that I came in." Abel turned his eyes down and waited for me to reply.

"I saw the shopkeeper the day you got here, Abel," I said. "Remember, I went out that afternoon to buy food and the other clothing for you. He told me how he had found the store that morning and I thought that it might have been you."

I remembered for a moment the details of the theft, and I should have confronted Abel with them, but his tragic face and the memory of the bruises he had come with convinced me not to mention it.

"Why didn't you say anything?" he asked. This inspired me to a brilliant answer.

"I was waiting for you to tell me," I said. "You must have been frightened, alone in the rain and the dark."

"What about the shopkeeper?"

"I had already explained who I was buying the shirts for," I said, "and he could guess as well as I could who was likely to be the thief."

Abel took on an air of conspiratorial embarrassment that made us into an exclusive club. "Did you have to pay for what I took?"

"I offered," I said, "but he wouldn't take it."

Abel looked up at me with an expression that must thrill every parent: he recognized his error and he looked to me for guidance. "Should I go tell him I'm sorry?" he asked. This question won me over so completely that I felt almost inclined to think the shopkeeper had pissed on his own door.

"I think that would be very nice," I said. "Shall I go with you?"

Abel wanted to go immediately but he insisted on practicing his apology with me before we left. We did not go out the door until he was satisfied that his phrasing—and, I imagine, his demeanor—was perfect. The shopkeeper was a nice soft old man, and Abel looked so sad and downtrodden when we walked in that he was reluctant even to hear an apology.

Abel explained in detail how he came to his forced entry and theft, all while carefully emphasizing that he did not seek with his explanation to excuse himself or deny responsibility. He promised that he would pay for everything he had taken as soon as he had some money to call his own, although he could not say when that would be. Only after a small polite argument did he accept the shopkeeper's gift of the stolen clothing.

"May I wait outside?" he asked when he had finished.

"That's a very bright boy you've got there," the old man said after Abel had gone. "Where did he come from?"

"He just showed up at my door," I said. The old man shook his head and laughed. "I guess everyone gets a chance," he said.

I joined my bright boy on the porch after buying a few things and we began the walk home.

"It was kind of him to make me a present of the clothes," Abel said unhappily, "but if I don't pay for what I took I won't ever feel like I've made it up."

"I could insist on paying for them," I said. You see I already took it for granted that it was my place to provide for him.

"But *I* stole them," Abel snapped.

"I really don't think you can pay someone for something if he won't take your money," I said. "I think you should just forget about it. I want to introduce you to my friend Diana, and I'd like to have Dr. Ericsson over for dinner—why don't I invite them both and make it a party?"

Abel turned his face slightly down and watched me from the corner of his eye. "What did the doctor say about me?" he asked.

"He didn't think that this was the first time you'd been beaten up."

"What else?"

"He said that you were very intelligent," I said. We had come to the green house and I unlocked the door. Abel grinned.

"He was right," I added.

"Nothing bad?"

"He also thought that you may have been sick before," I said.

Abel smiled. "All right," he said.

In my study I decided to write formal cards of invitation for Diana and the doctor. I asked them both to dinner two nights from that night. After writing out the cards, I realized that it would be ridiculous to mail them, since neither Dr. Ericsson nor Diana lived much further from me than the postbox. But I did not want to waste the cards, so I took a walk and slipped them under their doors.

I also set a formal table. Every place had its folded napkin and even its place card. Dr. Ericsson's wife, Lucy, was away that week so we were only four. I put Abel opposite Diana at my square table and myself to Diana's left, with the doctor to her right.

Since Abel had arrived I had been ignoring Diana, and she had only provisionally forgiven me. She did not return my friendly greeting when I met her outside my door.

"Here I am," she said.

"Thank you for coming," I answered. She stood before me in a dark green sweater and a navy blue skirt, her hair tied away behind her head, as if waiting to be touched. Diana has light green eyes and a few brown freckles on her pale white skin. Another man might not call her beautiful, but she has regular features and the sort of prettiness that in a young girl is attributed to youth. We stood silent for a moment.

"Where is he?" she asked, looking over my shoulder into the house. She wore perfume on her throat. "I want to see him."

"He's upstairs," I said.

Diana pushed me lightly out of her way and slid inside.

"Excuse me," she said pointedly. "Do I get to see him?"

"I'll ask him to come down when Dr. Ericsson gets here."

I shut the door. Diana stood staring at the staircase and spoke without turning around. "Hasn't he been examined already?"

"I invited the doctor to dinner."

"Oh," she said.

There was a knock on the door, and I opened it to see Michael.

"Good evening, Joseph," he said. He handed me a bottle of wine.

"This wasn't necessary," I said as I read the label. A knowledge of wine is one of the useless things I achieved incidentally to being a lawyer, and I saw that the doctor had not spared expense. I led him in with my head still bent over the bottle.

"Hello, Diana," he said smiling.

She smiled and took his hand. "Good evening, Dr. Ericsson," she said.

"Michael," he said.

"I'll go up and get Abel," I said. I touched Diana on the shoulder and ran up the stairs. I found Abel in my study reading, his hair damp and carefully combed, his shirt bright and buttoned.

"They're here," I said.

Abel put down the book and stood up hesitantly. "Do I look nice?" he asked. He did not look like a boy but like a young man.

"You look very handsome," I answered paternally. I brought him to the top of the stairs with my hand on his shoulder. In the living room he shook hands formally with both of the guests as I introduced him.

"Oh," he said as he met Diana, "you were right, Joseph."

Diana looked at me questioning and I shrugged.

"What was he right about?" she asked him.

"He said that you were beautiful."

The doctor smiled at this and Diana laughed.

"Are you training him for a ventriloquist act, Joseph?" she said.

Abel flushed briefly but then pressed on. "Is your name Greene with an *e*?" he asked.

Still laughing at me, Diana nodded.

"But her middle name," I said to her, "is Green without an *e*."

She compressed her eyebrows at me—her repetitive name embarrasses her.

"Your parents must have been a perfect match," Abel said. I turned my attention back to him. Such remarks to Diana could hardly sound natural, but his age and evident sincerity made them endearing. At least I thought so; Diana thanked him without quite paying attention.

"And you'll remember Dr. Ericsson," I said.

"Good evening, sir," Abel said to him. Dr. Ericsson nodded

and continued to smile. Abel looked at him as if they shared a secret, and then turned to address me.

"I don't think I was a very good patient," he said. He turned back to the doctor and said, "I hope you will forgive me."

The doctor's smile broadened, but I did not understand its character. "I am a professional," he said.

All parties paused.

"Shall we sit down?"

I think that it will be more profitable to record my impressions of the evening than to try to reconstruct all our conversation over dinner. That would go on for thousands of words and, in black ink, remain flat, and the dinner was not flat. If anything it was lopsided. The doctor, first of all, smiled and spoke from time to time, but for the most part sat straight and quiet, and I, for my part, liked to listen. But once the young man had a glass of wine in him, he began speaking at a speed that I could hardly keep up with, and Diana, also slightly drunk and always more outgoing than I am, followed him easily.

His mind was inexhaustible. He spoke with the rapid enthusiasm and quick changes of youth but with the verbal and intellectual sophistication of age. But he could say almost nothing that Diana did not have an answer for; some of these answers were at his expense, but Abel either did not notice or else took them in stride, talking over and past them.

At one point Diana began to cough and excused herself to get a glass of water. The table was silent for a moment. The doctor looked at me, cleared his throat, and asked Abel what he thought of Bettley so far. Abel had little to say about Bettley in particular, but what he did say led him directly to talking about small towns in general. The doctor made some remark ostensibly making fun of people who live in small towns but really directed at Abel's affected worldliness. Abel, whether through density or courtesy, took the doctor's remark at face value and expanded on it, reaching a degree of absurdity that made me and the doctor begin laughing as Diana came back to the table. When we looked at her expectantly she said something about all of humanity's ills coming from its cities, and Abel took off again, creating a debate of *urbs* v. *rus* that even drew in the doctor. When I was asked, as a man who had lived in both, what I thought, everyone waited politely for me to air my considered views. I said that I thought that the country was better suited to childhood and old age.

"I guess you and Diana have both ends covered," Abel said. This is a good example of why it is better to recount this conversation indirectly—somehow at the time this remark sounded amusing. (I am eleven years older than Diana.)

"You are an old, old man, Joseph," Diana said.

From city and country Abel tumbled to the legitimacy of the nation-state, finally drawing in the doctor. Diana, on the other hand, began playing with her napkin, and I stopped putting in even my occasional words. I had been a lawyer, it is true, but never since law school had I had occasion to deal with the larger principles of my field, and I found myself with nothing to add. Abel and the doctor agreed that every nation is ultimately founded on force and coercion, but they disagreed about whether this completely undermined the nation's claims to community and commonwealth.

If I had stopped speaking, though, I do not mean to say that I was bored; I was not, I was fascinated. I was interested in the conversation, I was interested in the doctor's views, and I was fascinated by the bright young man who spoke so quickly. His speech only faltered for the first time after we had all finished eating. Abel insisted that an institution founded on coercion could have no true benevolence.

"You will discover," the doctor said, "when you are older— at least I hope you will—that institutions, like the people that make them up, can be good and bad at the same time."

"When I'm older?" Abel said, reverting to the half-serious tone he had most often been using. "I don't see . . ."

But the doctor was refolding his napkin and setting his silverware across his plate. Abel trailed off and the conversation with him.

When I returned from the kitchen with a blueberry pie for dessert, Abel turned his wit on me. He asked me what sort of apron I wore when I baked; then Diana asked me if it had frills on it, and then Abel asked if it was pink. Finally Dr. Ericsson looked at his watch.

"How much sleep do you get, Abel?" he said.

Abel was caught off guard. "Maybe seven hours," he said. It was usually ten hours between the time he closed his bedroom door in the evening and the time I woke him in the morning. I guessed that he, like me, liked to read in bed.

"You should have at least ten," Dr. Ericsson said with finality. "Ten hours a night for anyone your age, and particularly for you."

Abel affected his half-serious expression and looked away from the grave doctor in joking appeal to me. I smiled at him but I did not take his side.

"He's the doctor," I said.

Abel took his defeat like a gentleman. "All right," he said. "Good night, Dr. Ericsson. Good night, Joseph. Good night, Diana Green Greene."

He walked out of the room with his plate.

2

Diana stirred sugar into her coffee. "What an obnoxious child," she said. I thought of Abel alone in his room and imagined him nervously wondering how my friends had liked him, or happily remembering how well they had all gotten along, and I stiffened and did not reply. I had not had a chance to speak to the doctor.

"How are your cases?" I asked him.

"I had a very difficult case today," he answered me. He sounded tired and he let his gaze fall down to the table. Diana looked up and watched the doctor with concern.

"In town?" I asked.

"I was in Penley," he said. Penley is the closest large town to Bettley. The doctor sighed and looked into his coffee.

"It was a child who had fallen," he said at last. "They said they didn't remember how or where. I think it might have been out a window."

"Just today?"

"No," he said, "at least a couple of months ago. He didn't seem to have anything worse than a bump on the head at the time so they didn't call anyone."

He stopped speaking again.

"Why now?" I said.

"They think that he's acting differently."

"How old is he?"

"He's only four," the doctor said, "and the last time I saw him he had barely started speaking."

"What do they say is different?"

"They say that he used to be very shy, but he isn't anymore; he came right up to me and asked me my name when I came in. The grandmother thinks his eyes look hollow."

"Malnourishment?"

"Spiritually hollow," he said. "Anyway, there were no gross neurological deficits, and he seemed perfectly intelligent and functional. I told them."

"They didn't believe you?"

"We were talking at cross-purposes—they insisted that he'd changed, but since I hadn't seen him in so long, and since their description of the change was so vague, I couldn't look for anything but something wrong."

"Maybe he was emotionally injured by his parents' letting him fall out a window," Diana said.

"It's possible," the doctor said. "I don't really suspect them of anything, though, and if none of them even remember what happened, what can I say?"

"Nothing," I said.

"Finally I told them that I had done everything I could do, and that if they remained concerned they would have to go to the hospital."

"I don't see what else you could have done," I said; Diana said something similar.

"It's just hard to think that this child may very well spend the rest of his life with the idea that he isn't himself. I honestly think the grandmother believes he's been switched for a fairy changeling."

"If they talk about it enough maybe they'll manage to make him shy again," I said.

"It's not impossible," he said.

He looked at his watch and stood up. "Well, Joe," he said, "I think I'd better go home and straighten up before my wife gets home."

Diana asked, "Where has she been?"

"She went to stay with her family in the city for a few days," he said. "She's in her second month and she wants to visit them as much as she can before she's far enough along that I start insisting she stay home."

Diana laughed. "Lucy will go when she wants to," she said.

Michael smiled. "She may humor me," he said.

I stood up and walked him to the door.

"Listen," he said to me, "Joseph, I'm sorry to have been a poor guest tonight."

"What?"

"I've just been—"

"Maybe he's just learning to overcome his family," I said, and the doctor stopped.

"I hadn't thought of that," he said. He smiled. "I hope that's it."

"It was a pleasure to have you."

"I insist," he answered, "that the pleasure was mine."

"We'll do it again," I said, and we shook hands.

"Good night, Diana!" he called out.

"Good night, Dr. Ericsson!" she yelled back.

I saw the doctor to the door and then returned to sit with Diana.

"Did you have an all-right time tonight?" I asked.

"I had an all-right time, Joseph."

"I'm glad you got along with Abel so well."

"Someone had to talk to him," she said. "You were just sitting there like an old man."

"I thought we had established that I *was* an old man."

"Oh, that's right," Diana said. "Abel and I got along because we're in the same age-group."

"Also," I said, "I enjoyed discussing the frills on my apron."

"It's just so naturally fascinating, Joseph, I couldn't help myself."

"Do you want any more coffee?"

She shook her head. We sat without speaking and I heard in my ears the buzzing of the quiet night. I became suddenly aware of Diana's body across the table from mine, her real shoulders beneath the green sweater, the texture of the sweater, the underside of her chin. But in the same moment I was aware of Abel's body in his bedroom above us, his dark young face in innocent sleep, and one of the bodies made me ashamed before the other, though I did not know which.

"Diana—"

"I think I'm going to go, Joseph," she said and stood up. "Do you need any help cleaning up first?"

"Oh. No, that's all right. I can do it."

"Good night," she said.

I watched her walk out. She did not turn but walked straight to the door and out. For several minutes I sat unmoving, looking first at the door and then at my hands. Finally I stood up and began to clear the dishes, but I quickly lost patience with this and decided to go to bed.

Upstairs I opened the door to the guest room and stood for a long time in the doorway watching Abel sleep. He slept on his back with a sheet pulled up to his throat and he hardly moved; I could scarcely see him breathe. Nevertheless his body somehow gave the impression of trembling or pulsing, as if his blood flowed fiercely beneath his quiet skin.

In my own bed I lay awake for hours, turning and sweating, unable to sleep.

3

By the time I got downstairs in the morning, Abel had fed himself and was reading in the living room.

"I'll wash the dishes when I finish this chapter," Abel said.

"That's all right," I said, intending to wash them myself but forgetting it as soon as I had spoken the words. I picked up a book from the shelf—something about the sexual vectors of consumption—and lay down on the couch.

"I didn't sleep very well," I told Abel. "If I fall asleep now, just wake me up when you want to eat lunch."

"All right," Abel said, laughing. I did not know what he thought was funny, but I did not ask him since I fell asleep immediately. When I woke up it was almost one o'clock and I was alone in the living room. I found Abel in my study looking through my microscope; I stopped in the doorway.

"What are you looking at?" I asked.

"Something fatal," he said.

"Be careful." I had never let anyone use my microscope before. "I'm going to make lunch," I said after a minute, and went back downstairs. By the time Abel joined me a few minutes later, I felt awake.

"Why didn't you sleep well?" Abel said.

"I don't know," I answered. "Sometimes at my age you don't."

He smiled at this as he walked across the kitchen. "You're not that old," he said. He took his place next to me at the counter, and as I moved around assembling ingredients for sandwiches he took things from my hands and organized them neatly.

"Was it because Diana was here?" he said. "Did she stay over?"

"How old are you, Abel?"

"Never mind," he said, smiling discreetly, and our reactions seemed so much at odds with our relative ages and positions that I laughed.

"Too old," I said, "however old you are. Where is the—"

Abel handed me the bread knife.

"She didn't stay over?" he said.

"No, Abel," I said, "she went home and went to bed."

"Isn't she your girlfriend?" Abel asked.

"Why?" I said. "Do you have an interest?"

"I'm just asking, Joseph."

I pointed the bread knife at him and tried to make a joke.

"You'd better watch your step, cowboy," I said. Abel laughed at me and brought the food to the table. I cleared my throat and changed the subject.

"I'm glad that you got along with the doctor," I said.

"He's very intelligent."

"He said the same thing about you," I said.

"I know."

Eventually, once we stopped talking about the dinner party, our conversation picked up. In the end we spent half the afternoon sitting at the table. We talked, among other things, about the sexual vectors of consumption—Abel had read through my book while I was asleep. Abel made an interesting point about the moral implications of catching tuberculosis from a prostitute: a man so infected, if he is ashamed of seeing a prostitute, will not be able to admit that he is sick, and so will be dragged by the one shameful act into shamefully infecting his family— evil propagates evil.

His conversation with me could be every bit as fast and exciting as had been his conversation with Diana at dinner: I liked to imagine that he simply thought in rapid, massive waves. It did not seem to matter very much that I was not as quick as Diana; indeed, in speaking to Abel, I felt as if I were, because I was dragged along by the current of his speech.

Earlier I referred to the "heroic month of July." What I meant by this was that just as my own thoughts and remarks seemed quicker and brighter when in the current of Abel's, so too did my life as a whole seem quicker and brighter. I woke up one morning to take a walk in the forest and, finding Abel awake, brought him with me. The purity of reverence that I found in his eyes as we walked under the tallest pines filled me with rapture; when I later mentioned my fantasy of the trees as parliamentarians he took over the idea and expanded it so rapidly—making the clouds a house of commons, the squirrels popular tribunes, the floor of dead needles the weight of precedent, and the earth itself the constitutional queen—that I was giddy. I came to depend on Abel for the day's entertainment and transportation; his most passing thought became a revelation.

Only toward the end of the month did I begin to realize how much I had been neglecting my friends Diana and Dr. Ericsson, and only then did I begin to consider that I was unlikely to be as fascinating to Abel as he was to me. The best solution to both problems was another dinner party. I took a walk late one afternoon to invite my friends and then returned home to make Abel dinner.

"I'm afraid that this must have been a boring month for you," I said to him.

"I like talking to you, Joseph," he said. "You have an open mind."

Abel was sitting at the table in a white shirt open at the neck, and his thick dark hair was combed back away from his eyes. He was healthier now, and his face had taken back what is called an olive cast of skin. His dark brown eyes had surface tints of gray and green. He looked like a young prince.

"Thank you," I said, unduly pleased with the compliment and myself.

"Nevertheless," I said, once having brought myself back, "I thought you might enjoy another dinner party. I invited Diana and the doctor to come over on Friday."

"All right," Abel said, "I'm glad."

On Friday night Diana and the doctor arrived at my door at the same time and Abel let them in. I watched from the doorway of the kitchen, where I had a pan on the stove that I did not want to leave.

Diana came in first, and I was surprised to see that she had dressed up. She was wearing a pearl gray tailored jacket over a white blouse, a matching knee-length skirt, and black stockings. She shook Abel's hand heartily and then stood awkwardly aside as he shook hands with the doctor.

Abel asked the doctor a question that I could not hear and then they two turned slightly away from Diana as the doctor put one hand on the boy's shoulder and gestured with the other. Diana crossed the room to say hello to me in the kitchen.

"You look so cute in your apron!" she exclaimed. "That's why we're all so fascinated," she added. It was a quilted blue apron that she had picked out for me one day when we had met at the store. Diana looked beautiful.

"You look very nice, too," I said. "What do you have holding back your hair?"

She turned around to show me a tortoiseshell comb that she said she had inherited from her grandmother. I glanced back at the range; Diana leaned down to pull a loose thread off my shirt. I touched her lightly.

"Sit down, Diana," I said. "Michael," I called out, "Abel, sit down! The leeks are translucent."

"Oh, we'd better hurry then," I heard Abel say. I carried out the hot pans hastily and walked around the table to serve. While I was doing this Dr. Ericsson stood up and went into the kitchen for a corkscrew. He uncorked the bottle of wine that he had brought and poured us each a full glass.

"It's helping to bring out Abel's color," he said.

I put away my apron and sat down. I raised my glass. "To life in a small town," I said.

"And those that live it," Diana added.

"Yes," Abel said, histrionic and loud, "to small-town folk, God bless them!"

Diana put down her glass; the doctor and I drank.

I began to ask the doctor whether he had had any interesting new cases, but Abel interrupted me. "Cases!" Abel said. "We can't talk about cases. Something else, someone suggest something else!"

"Are you already drunk, Abel?" the doctor asked.

"I am drunk, my dear doctor," Abel replied, tossing his head back and raising his hands in a perfect imitation of an expansive drunken gesture, "on the glorious summertime!"

"Maybe you should put away the wine, Joseph," Diana said.

"Let old women cling to temperance," Abel recited, "but drink is for the young!"

Diana looked stunned and everyone fell silent; I served the food. Abel held out his plate with a curt nod, and the doctor passed me his plate and Diana's. Abel wet his lips and began speaking.

He started with a disquisition on the moral nature of man, using the seasons of the year as a framework. He supplied himself with questions, answers, and suggestions as he went along. He stopped aside to talk about the wine, and then returned to the seasons with a manic speech about the winter of the soul:

the soul, he submitted to our gracious consideration, as he said, did not live to be more than one year old—it began in childish spring, and if it precociously reached an early winter, then there in the winter it would remain.

Here Diana spoke. "That's ridiculous, Abel," she said.

"Aha!" Abel said, his face red and shining. "Have I succeeded in awakening you? Have I roused an argument? Tell me, Miss Greene, in which particular am I wrong?"

"You're just talking out of the side of your mouth," Diana said.

"That's very colorful," Abel said. "What does it mean?"

"It means you're full of hot air," she said.

"I'm full of hot blood," he answered.

"You're full of wine," she said.

"She's got you there, Abel," the doctor said.

"She doesn't," Abel said. "She hasn't answered my question."

"That's true," Diana said.

"Because you don't know."

"Because I don't *care*," Diana said.

"Is there any difference?"

"I don't know *and* I don't care," Diana said. "It's getting late, Joseph."

"No," I said, "it's not that late," and Abel began talking about the nature of knowledge and its relationship to volition. The doctor turned his eyes to his plate and Diana's expression developed from boredom through irritation toward hostility. But I was entranced. I thought that Abel had blossomed and I took pleasure in listening to him. Here, I thought, is the company that the boy has wanted for.

This is not to say that I was oblivious to Diana's expressions or without any discomfort of my own at Abel's domination of the conversation. But I was still, as I have said, the same sort of "good person" I had been in the city: accommodating to others at my own expense. It was not a question of my consciously dismissing my discomfort, or of rebuking myself for resenting Abel; the dismissal was so automatic that I was hardly aware of the resentment in the first place. I was able, therefore, to feel resentment toward Abel even as he fascinated me, and both of these even as I felt apprehension and guilt toward Diana, and no one feeling interfered with any other.

This time Abel did not even allow himself to be sent to bed: he preempted it. I was just getting up to bring out dessert when Abel interrupted himself to ask the doctor the time. "Tell me, good doctor," he said, "do you carry a timepiece?"

The doctor looked at his watch before holding it out to show Abel. Abel leaned over it like a nearsighted old man before thanking the doctor with an inappropriate and insincere effusion and standing up. He bowed theatrically to the doctor, to Diana, and to me in the kitchen door.

"Having been previously well instructed," he said, "that a child of my age must have abundant sleep, I will leave you for the night."

He spun a circle on the floor and then glided to the stairs.

"Finally," Diana said.

I carried out a tray with cake and coffee and sat down. The doctor leaned forward and set out all the coffee cups as Diana turned on me. "Why don't you do something about him, Joseph?" she demanded.

"What about him?"

"He needs to learn how to behave," Diana said.

"What did he do?"

Diana looked to the doctor but the doctor was looking away.

"He insulted me, Joseph!"

Diana was glaring at me but I would not meet her eyes.

"He was only joking," I said.

"I know the difference—"

"It wasn't so terrible," I said, staring into the corner. "I don't know why you're so upset."

The doctor cleared his throat.

"Can I pour you some coffee, Diana?" he said.

"No, thank you, doctor," she said. She stood up abruptly and with an awful scraping of her chair. "I'm going home."

Diana walked out. Dr. Ericsson poured two cups of coffee.

"Never mind, Joseph," he said, "it's all the more for us."

CHAPTER FIVE

1

On the first day of August I awoke early. For the first time in weeks I had made plans for the day that did not include, much less depend on, Abel. I was going to go into the pine forest alone for several hours. I would walk among the trees in communion with them. I think I had begun to realize, if not in so many words, that I missed myself as much as I missed Diana or Dr. Ericsson. Diana I had not seen since she stormed out of dinner, so sometime before the middle of the day I planned to go knock on her door and convince her to take a walk with me. Then perhaps later in the afternoon I would drop by my friend's office and see if he was in.

"Good morning," Abel said sleepily from the doorway. I was in the kitchen, having milked the cow and eaten my breakfast, packing my small bag. "Where are you going?"

He seemed young and helpless, and I remembered, not really with shame, but certainly with some embarrassment, that I had intended to leave him alone in the house all day without warning.

"I was going to go—"

"Aren't we going to eat breakfast?" he said.

I did not know how to answer this and stood blankly for a moment. I could see his thin white shoulders; I had already eaten my breakfast; I felt ashamed of being so irresponsible but disinclined to break my plan. "Well," I said, "I guess . . ."

"Can I have eggs?" he said. He sounded so innocent and trusting as he said this—so trusting of me—that it nearly cracked my heart into pieces.

"You can have whatever you want," I said. I walked across the kitchen to turn on the light and then back again to open the cupboard for a pan.

"Scrambled, please," Abel said, sitting back in his chair.

Again I stood undecided for a moment before settling again that it would be easiest simply to make him his eggs before I left. "All right," I said. I put my bag down and turned on a burner on the stove.

"Can I have tea, also?" he asked. I turned on another burner.

Abel sat at the table thinking with grave concentration about I know not what while I made and served him breakfast. By the time I had done this it was full daylight. I put down his plate and cup in the sink and picked up my bag.

"What are we going to do today?" he asked.

"Well," I said slowly, the bag trailing from my fingers, "as for myself, I was thinking of going into the pine forest."

I stood and waited for Abel to answer.

"All right," he said, "but I need a few minutes to get dressed."

Once again I stood blankly. I looked at my watch; Abel stood up and put his dishes in the sink. I opened my mouth to explain that I did not want him to go.

"I'll wash it when we get back," he said, and somehow that defeated me. I think that I may even have slumped a little.

"I wanted to go before it got too hot," I said weakly, and Abel stood up straighter and smiled.

"I won't take too long," he said and walked out of the room.

I sat down at the table and dropped my bag on the floor. I believe that the first thing I thought of was an image of Diana's straight nose in profile against the dark green background of the pines. I looked at my watch and imagined telling Abel that I had a date with her. But I did not even know whether she was home and I did not like to lie to him. Then I told myself that at least we could drop by the doctor's office, but I knew how that would turn out. Abel would come along and begin talking, and the doctor, willing neither to participate in the conversation nor to be the one to quiet him, would simply excuse himself. He would have a patient. Then I thought of the tall and silent pines that would not speak to me when I brought a chattering friend.

After ten minutes of sitting at the table I decided to clean up the breakfast and I stood up. I washed Abel's plate and teacup and put them in the drying rack. I washed the frying pan. I wiped the table. This all took ten minutes or more at my reluctant slow speed. I sat down again and looked at my watch for several minutes.

"Abel!" I yelled. He did not answer. I walked to the foot of the stairs and yelled his name again.

"I'm coming," he answered. I thought of going upstairs to see why it was taking him so long, but what if he wasn't dressed? I did not want to be confronted by his thin white shoulders again. I did not want to see the flabby muscle hanging from his chest. He was too young for that.

I carefully resolved not to look at my watch or to think about the sun mounting up the sky. But nothing else interested me at that moment, so by a process of elimination I found myself sitting in my kitchen sullenly trying to meditate. I do not know how long I did it: on the one hand, it is hard to imagine that I had any success with that sort of bitter concentration; on the other hand, it seems unlikely to me that Abel would have come down directly after saying that he would.

In any case, when he came into the kitchen he found me sitting at the table with my chin in my hands, half forgetful of the pine forest. I did not really look up as he strode around packing himself food and drink into my bag. He put the bag down on the table before me and slammed out the door.

"Come on!" he shouted behind him. "It's already hot!"

I stood up and picked up the heavy bag. I hurried out the back door. It took me twice as long as usual to lock the lock because I was trying to hurry; Abel was moving quickly out of sight, and he would not know how to find his way back.

It had always been my custom to enter the forest formally. Sometimes I would stop at the edge and bid a good morning to the tree nearest my right hand and the tree nearest my left. Sometimes I would execute a sort of turning bow that took in all the trees I could see. Sometimes I recited an extemporaneous poem. Most frequently I would simply stand silently for a moment with my eyes closed.

This time I ran into the wood so quickly that I almost went the wrong way and lost sight of Abel, but he was luckily wearing a red shirt that I caught sight of from the corner of my eye.

"Abel," I shouted, *"wait!"* and he stopped walking until I had almost reached him. I stopped for a moment to catch my breath and then after coming abreast of him I started to speak.

He interrupted. "Do you ever go off that way?" he said.

"I think it's pretty much the same in all directions from here," I said.

"All right," he said, "let's go that way, then."

I looked off to the right, for a moment tempted, before I fell in with him to the left.

I did get my silence in a way. We walked for over an hour without speaking. But when I walked in the forest alone, I wandered slowly and paid no attention to where I was going. I was always confident of finding my way back and I never went too far in any case. But now I was worried about being separated from Abel, who could get lost, and I found myself paying most of my attention to the problem of remaining next to him.

He walked more quickly than is necessary in a morning walk through the forest, but I could not get him to slow down. Once I asked him, and he did slow down graciously, but before long he regained his speed. I tried simply slowing my own pace, just as I sometimes tried turning this or the other way from his path, but in every case he continued walking in his own direction at his own pace and I invariably gave up and matched myself to him.

There was something violent in the way Abel walked. I do
not mean that he looked ready to attack me or the pine trees, or
even that his feet hit the ground harder than they should have.
Somehow his body seemed to me to tremble with excess
energy, an energy that tended outwards. He looked older in his
red shirt, and he had combed his hair forward; he looked like
the son of a rich family on a hunting expedition. He walked
with his hands in his pockets.

"I'm hungry," he said. He stopped suddenly and I walked a
few steps past him and then doubled back. "Are you ready to
stop walking and have lunch?" he asked.

Something about his question bothered me and I said no.
"I'd rather keep walking awhile," I said.

"All right," he answered, "let me take my things out of the
bag and I'll find you after I eat."

"You'll find me?"

"Or I'll just meet you back at the house."

He smiled. I did not see the point of saying anything; if he
thought he knew where he was but I did not think he did, it was
clearly my obligation to accommodate him. We had reached a
clearing around a small slope. I sat down and leaned against the
slope as I opened the bag.

"So I'm not going to meet you?" he said. He was still standing up. "You're going to eat now?"

"I'll eat now," I said.

"I think my things are on top." He took the bag out of my
hands. He took out a sandwich that he had made himself and
the half bottle of wine that I had put into the bag for myself.

"Where's the corkscrew?" he said, handing me back the bag.

I put the bag down, the better to get at my own food, and ignored his question. He remained standing over me waiting. I took out my own bread and cheese and set them in my lap; I thrust out my hand holding the corkscrew toward Abel. He opened and began to drink my wine.

"Aren't you going to sit down?" I said.

"I like to eat standing up."

He wandered around in the small clearing as he ate and drank, stopping on the far end for a moment and putting the bottle down in the dirt. I took my knife out of the bag and sliced the bread and cheese.

"I wonder what's on the other side of this," Abel said. He put his half-eaten sandwich in the bag and walked past me up the slope.

"Don't get lost," I said.

"I'll be right back."

I wanted to get up and retrieve the wine bottle but I could not move without disturbing the food I had carefully laid out across my lap. I ate it dry, and by the time I had finished Abel returned. He returned from the opposite direction.

"I thought I would be able to see the house from up there," Abel said. He stooped down to pick up the wine bottle. "But I couldn't see anything—I realized I have no idea where I am."

I stood up and brushed the crumbs from my pants.

"Here," he said, handing me the bottle. It was about a quarter full. Abel brushed off his own clean clothing.

"Which way do you want to go back?" he said. "The same way or circle around?"

I packed up the bag. I did not want to go back, but I decided that it would be easier not to say anything; then, too, if I took him home, I could come back out by myself.

"We'll go this way," I said, starting to walk. I set off at a quick pace, hoping to put Abel in the uncomfortable following position that I had been in, but again he managed to take over: he strolled along carelessly and stopped often to examine tree bark. I was not yet willing to lose him in the forest, so again I matched my pace to his.

Eventually we reached the green house, and as I unlocked the back door I decided to say something; I do not know quite what it would have been.

"Abel," I began, and he interrupted.

"I've got some things to do this afternoon, Joe," he said. "I'm afraid you'll be on your own."

With that he slipped past me through the door and went upstairs. I cleaned out the bag in the kitchen.

2

I went directly to Diana's house in town. I passed one or two acquaintances and shortly said hello and then I knocked on Diana's door. She opened the door and stood in the threshold with her hair halfway out of its comb and strands floating in the air around her face. She wore a white apron and there may have been white flour on her hands.

"Hello, Joseph," she said pleasantly. Her eyes were green.

"Diana," I said, "I want to tell you—"

I choked. I felt a terrible compulsion to declare myself to Diana, but without being sure quite what I wanted to declare, and having no idea what to say.

She stood looking at me. "Joseph," she said, "I'm baking."

"Please," I said, "Diana—"

I coughed several times and then stood silently, holding up my hand, waiting to catch my breath. Although she was no less beautiful than always, Diana also seemed to me no less forbidding than beautiful. I was half inclined to say good-bye and go home, but I thought of Abel's dark eyes in the living room and I did not want to see them yet.

"I'm baking, Joseph, and I was just about to—"

"Diana," I said, approaching her suddenly and awkwardly. She stepped quickly out of the way and began to laugh.

"Joseph," she said, laughing, looking from me to her kitchen door and back, "the cake is burning."

"Diana," I said roughly, grabbing her by the shoulders; she twisted away from my grip and ran into the kitchen. I heard the bang of the oven and then smelled smoke; the cake must have caught fire. Whatever violence had taken hold of me disappeared completely. I called out some apology to Diana in the kitchen, but she did not answer. I thought that I could hear her scraping the cake off into the sink as I left.

Abel was not talking when I returned home. Here again I think English suffers for lack of a word: I want to say in Latin, for example, *tacebat*, that he was actively silent. For he was not ignoring me, and he was not sullen, but merely silent in such a fashion that I did not feel I could talk. I did not, in any case, have anything to say.

The next evening I asked him to help me cook dinner. I was going to make spaghetti and I did not need any help, but for his sake—so I said to myself—he should take a role in the maintenance of the house. It would help him become responsible.

He was sitting in the living room reading a history of sanatoria and he looked up from his book patiently.

I stood over him hesitantly. "Abel," I said, "do you want to help me with dinner tonight?"

He smiled. "I don't think so, Joseph, thank you," he said. "I'd like to finish my book."

Now I smiled patiently. "I'm sorry," I said, "I meant to say, will you please help me make dinner tonight?"

"Oh," he said, pressing his eyebrows together as if I had said something odd. "All right."

He put down his book on the couch and followed me into the kitchen.

"What do you want me to do?" he asked. I did not know what to tell him at first, but then I produced some onions for him to chop. He approached them as if he had no idea what to do with them, so I suggested that he take the outside layers off first. This did not seem to help him, so I interrupted what I was doing to demonstrate. I took off the outside layers and chopped off the ends.

"Now just chop it into small pieces," I said. I returned to the stove and put up a pot of water to boil. When I looked back to Abel I saw that instead of cutting the onion into pieces he was methodically slicing small bits from the edges. I stared at him.

"Abel," I said, "why don't you cut them into quarters first?"

He glanced at me and did not reply but began to cut the onion like a normal person. I quickly chopped some garlic and left myself with nothing to do. When Abel had finished chopping, he looked at me standing there and then went to the sink to rinse his hands.

"Thank you, Joseph," he said, walking out. "I enjoyed that."

"Abel," I said. He stopped and turned around. "Tomatoes."

Abel rolled his eyes and came back into the kitchen. I did not make him chop tomatoes for very long: he managed to squeeze all the juice from the pieces he cut onto the counter.

"All right," I said finally, "go read your book. I'll call you when dinner's ready." He silently washed his hands and returned to the living room.

He was perfectly pleasant when he came to the table. "Thank you," he said warmly as I served him. "Joseph," he said, when I had served myself and sat down, "do you still have any of your paintings?"

"What paintings?"

"Didn't you say that you wanted to be a painter when you were young?"

"Yes."

"So do you still have any?"

"No."

There was a minute's silence before the next question while Abel ate and I moved spaghetti around my plate.

"But what were they like?"

I looked at him hostilely and snapped out my answer. "I never painted anything, Abel."

"You mean you only made drawings?"

I did not answer this. I stared at Abel, trying to find deliberate malice in his eyes, but it was, if there, perfectly concealed. Innocently he persisted.

"You didn't try copying Mondrian?"

"What would be the point of copying a Mondrian?"

I continued to move my food in a circle around my plate; Abel, on the other hand, had no trouble eating between questions.

"One of the early ones, I mean," he said.

"It was an aspiration, Abel, more than a vocation."

"I'm sorry," he said with unnecessary emotion.

"All right—what about you?"

"What about me?" he said.

"What do you want to do? Are you interested in painting?"

"Oh," he said, smiling in embarrassment as if at a social error. "No," he said at last, "I'm not especially interested in painting."

"For any special reason?"

"I'm not interested in making unique objects."

"Would you rather design chairs for mass production?"

"No," he said, being patient with me, "I mean as art. I think it's ridiculous that a man can be a famous painter after he's dead on the basis of sixteen physical objects that could all fit in one furnace."

I imagined a furnace full of Vermeer and my hands began to tremble.

"Perhaps," I said with a calm full of effort, "you would rather write books?"

Abel laughed derisively. "Writing isn't art," he said. "It's fake. I guess I would compose masses if I had to choose an 'art.'"

"You don't have to 'choose an art,' Abel," I snapped. "I just asked you what you wanted to do. It's an open question."

Abel prodded his spaghetti casually, now fully in command of the conversation. "I want to do whatever I want," he said.

I sighed theatrically. "Brilliantly evaded," I said. I meant it as an aside—not one that he would not hear, but one that he would not bother to answer—but he decided to take offense.

"I'm not evading the question, Joseph," he said, "I'm answering it seriously. How old do you think I am? Are you planning to find me a master carpenter to apprentice to?"

He made me feel ashamed. I was an adult, after all, and he was a child.

"I was only trying to make conversation," I said.

"Some people," he said pointedly, "*never* figure out what to do with their lives."

"There's a difference," I said, "between making the wrong choice and—"

"Moreover," he said, "I have observed in the course of my life that it is generally the very people who are most uncertain of themselves that insist that others know exactly what they want. How old do you think I am?"

The doctor, I think, would have simply laughed at the spectacle of this teenage boy talking so belligerently about what he had "observed in the course of his life," but I did not laugh.

"Abel," I said, "look—"

"Can we just forget it?" he said. "Let's just eat."

"I'm sorry, Abel," I said, "but—"

"Let's just eat," he repeated, so we just ate.

After dinner Abel placed his dish in the sink and walked upstairs to his room. After I had cleaned up, I went into my study. I wanted to read my *Social History of Leprosy in Continental Europe,* but I could not find it. It was not on the shelf where I thought I remembered putting it, and I did not see it anywhere else. Finally I sat down at my desk and leafed through a book of Mondrian reproductions until it was time to go to sleep.

The next morning when I awoke I was, for some reason, embarrassed: I walked hesitantly into the kitchen hoping that Abel would not be there. But he was, sitting at the table, reading the newspaper.

"Good morning," I said, and Abel nodded shortly.

"I'm just going to go out to the shed and milk the cow," I said, and he glanced at the clock.

"All right, but can we have breakfast soon?"

"Sure," I said. I was trying to be especially friendly by way of an apology. "Do you have plans for the day?"

"I'm going to take the train into Penley and go to that bookstore you mentioned," he said, and I felt better.

"That's a nice idea," I said. "Will you be back for dinner?"

"Probably."

"Do you need any money?" I patted my pocket and remembered that my wallet was still on my dressing table. "I'll give you some money before you go."

Abel turned a page.

I walked out of the house and across the road to the shed. My cow, whom the eccentric old man had named Cassandra, lowed good morning. I rubbed her forehead.

"How are you this morning, Cassandra?" I said.

"Oh, much better now," I answered for her as milk began to hit the metal bucket.

"What have you heard from your son?" I asked. The most recent calf had been sold.

"Oh," she said, "he's raising hell and breaking hearts just like his daddy."

"Would you like me to make you breakfast, Cassandra?"

"That's all right, thank you," she said. "I've already eaten."

There was still plenty of hay.

"All right," I said, "thank you very much."

"No," I answered myself as I slipped through the door, "thank *you*."

As I put the milk away Abel was still reading the newspaper. I took out eggs and bacon and bread.

"Has anything happened in the world?" I asked.

"Nothing that hasn't happened before," he said.

Throughout breakfast he remained polite but cool, and I guiltily gave him twenty dollars for his trip and told him there would be food for him whenever he came home.

I walked with Abel as far as the store and then I let him continue alone. Inside the store I asked about roses.

"Trouble with Diana?" the shopkeeper said.

"Can't I just buy roses?"

"Sure you can," he said, but he did not have any. I do not actually like roses, especially, and I was just as happy to take three large sunflowers. They were at any rate more sincere than roses would have been.

I knocked on Diana's door but she did not answer or was not at home. The door was locked. I stood in front for a few minutes, thinking she might appear, but she did not; finally I left the flowers on the porch with a note. "Dear Diana," I wrote, "Please forgive me. I will make you a cake. Yours, Joseph."

3

Back in the house I flipped pointlessly through dictionaries until noon. I made myself lunch as slowly as I could, I ate lunch as slowly as I could, and I cleaned up after lunch as slowly as I could until finally, desperate to leave the house, I walked into town to the doctor's office.

Finding the door to the waiting room open I walked in and crossed the room to knock on his office door. I raised my hand to knock.

"What's the trouble?" Dr. Ericsson said. I turned around and saw him sitting in his waiting room with a magazine in his lap. "Have you killed the boy?"

I laughed.

"No," I said. He pointed to the other couch and I sat down.

"No," I said, "he's gone to Penley for the day. I just thought I would come say hello."

"I'm glad you did," the doctor said. He put down his magazine. "No one at all seems to be sick today. If I weren't the doctor I would go for a walk."

"You're not allowed to go for a walk?" I said. I was scandalized.

The doctor laughed. "I could go for a walk," he said. "But then I would lose the business if someone came in and died."

He put his feet up on the table. "The people of Bettley are too healthy," he said.

"Maybe we don't have enough smog."

"Too much fresh air," he said, counting on his fingers, "too much quiet, too much fresh food. It doesn't make for a very vibrant medical community."

"I guess it is very boring," I said. "You could always poison the water supply."

"The difficult thing," he said, "is to find a contaminant that will affect different people in different ways—an epidemic of a single problem is more work but it's not necessarily more interesting."

"Why stop at one contaminant?"

Dr. Ericsson laughed. "Why indeed," he said. "You know, I'm not entirely joking."

"Of course not."

"People always say that they become doctors to help people," he said. "I love to make people feel better, but as far as that goes, there are better ways of doing it if that's what you want—"

"Join the clergy," I said.

"Or start a trade union. But I'm really more interested in disease itself—my interest in people is entirely separate."

"How so?"

"You can personify disease," he said. "Imagine it as a shade creeping into your bones and your lungs, taking over your body, making you behave in a certain way, do certain things—"

"Fascinating," I said, laughing. In fact I rarely thought of disease as anything but an abstract metaphor and I thought the doctor's idea sounded awful.

"I think it is," he said.

"But why did you come up here?"

"I grew up in Penley," he said.

"I mean why didn't you go into the city? There must be more interesting death and decay there."

Dr. Ericsson shrugged and looked embarrassed. "I have trouble sleeping in the city," he said.

"When I moved up here," I told him, "it took me several weeks to get used to the crickets—the cicadas, whatever they are—I couldn't fall asleep. But now I think I would miss them."

Dr. Ericsson was a young man and I hated to think of him choosing the wrong direction or place for his life for a trivial reason.

"It isn't that," he said. "It's just the presence of so many other people—just knowing that they live and are all around me. I like that when I'm working, but I want to be alone at night."

"What about your wife?"

"Lucy's from the city," he said, "and she'll want to raise our children there, but until then she doesn't mind."

"I mean, does she sleep in the basement so that you can be alone at night?"

"Oh," he said, laughing, "I meant alone with her, Joe."

"I see."

We continued to talk about medical school and law school; I explained that I had gone to law school because my father was a lawyer and because I could not be a painter. He understood immediately what I meant by calling Mondrian's paintings perfect, and he said that it was terrible. He had not seen the work and I offered to show him reproductions.

"I'd be very interested," he said. "I've certainly seen paintings that I could conceive of no improvements on, but I can't imagine an artistic perfection of a kind that would exclude other perfections."

"I couldn't have either, before the show," I said. "But they didn't strike me that way immediately. Maybe I was only looking for an excuse to get out of an ambition that had gotten away from me."

I stood up.

"They *overshadow* painting, I would say, the way that a printed alphabet overshadows literature."

The doctor thought about this as I tied my shoes.

"An alphabet doesn't overshadow literature," he said. "It overshadows orthography."

I froze in my place for several seconds and finally laughed at myself.

"I wish you had said that when I was seventeen, Michael."

"Come visit again," he told me, and I walked out the door.

Walking back to the green house I thought about whether I agreed with the doctor. The alphabet has no existence apart from language. It can be used with many languages, but it must be used with one. On the other hand, the same thing is true the other way around— My thoughts were interrupted by the sight of Abel pacing back and forth in front of the house. "You locked the door!" he spat as soon as he saw me.

"Abel," I said, "I thought—"

"You locked the fucking door," he said, "and I don't have a fucking key!"

I had been starting to take my keys out of my pocket and my hand stopped halfway. "I'm sorry, Abel, I thought you were coming home later. I didn't think about it."

"Clearly you didn't think about it!" he shouted. His face was mottled and quickly intimidating me out of cool answers. "Is that an apology? I'm sorry, I burned your fucking house down—I didn't think about it. I'm sorry, I killed your fucking mother—I didn't think about it."

Uneasily I noticed the facility with which he said "burned your house down" and "killed your mother."

"Abel," I said, trying to put a hand on his shoulder. He threw it off.

"Listen to me, Abel," I said, falling back on the voice I had developed professionally to use on upset clients. "It was not an apology, it was only an explanation. But I am sorry—I am very sorry—that I made you wait, and that I didn't think about it, and that is an apology, all right? As soon as we go inside I'll give you the spare key."

"Why don't you give me your key?" he demanded.

"My key?"

"Because you don't like being locked out!"

I still had not opened the door. I was in fact somewhat frightened of the boy—there was a terrible violence in the way he spoke. But I had, despite my obscure place in my law firm, occasionally been in a room even with angry murderers, and I knew that it is important not to be provoked. I calmly unlocked and opened the door and held it open for Abel. He did not enter.

"Did you have to wait long?" I said.

"I've been here for hours," he said, and I congratulated myself that his voice, though still raised and angry, was no longer shouting.

"You can't have been here for hours, Abel," I said. I stepped into the house and held the door open. "It would have taken you two or three hours to make a round-trip to Penley even if you didn't leave the train station."

"Maybe I didn't go," Abel said, "how would you know? You went out and left the house locked up like a goddamned castle so I couldn't get in."

"Come inside, Abel," I said. "You know that I didn't mean to lock you out. And I was here all morning; I only went out after lunch."

Abel paced carefully into the hall, staring at me suspiciously.

"Did you have a good time in Penley?" I asked.

"No."

"Why not? Did you have trouble finding the bookstore?"

"Of course I had trouble finding the bookstore," he said, "it's on the other side of town! I had to ask four fucking old women how to get there!"

"There's nothing wrong with asking for directions," I said. We were standing in the entrance hall and I was leaning sideways and turning my body in an effort to coax Abel into the living room. "I've had to ask for directions in the city I grew up in."

"Is your being stupid supposed to make me feel better?"

I restrained myself from getting angry and simply walked into the living room. Abel followed me in.

"Did you see any interesting books?" I said. "I can see that you didn't buy any."

I sat down on the couch for a moment but, when Abel continued to pace, I stood up again.

"I saw lots of interesting books, Joseph," he said, and I allowed myself to believe that he was calming down. He began pacing back and forth in a straight line, and I sat down again.

"I saw many books of great interest," he said, speaking in a tight, emphatic voice through closed teeth. He did not look at me. "I saw a natural history of the buffalo. I saw an anthology of French short stories. I saw a new translation of an old epic."

I stood up and attempted to guide Abel gently into a seat: he threw my hands off his shoulders without breaking stride.

"Do you know," he said, "I even saw a book for you—*A Brief Study of Bovine Tuberculosis.*"

"Really?"

"I would have bought it for you, Joe," he said. "Ask me why I didn't."

Abel stopped walking and began rocking back and forth on his feet. He was by an end table, and his hands kept flicking up at the lamp that sat on it.

"Abel," I said, and he screamed; in fact I can say that he almost shrieked.

"Ask me why I didn't buy it for you!"

I fell back into the couch, astonished, frightened, and I gave in. "Why didn't you—"

He interrupted me by scooping the ceramic lamp from its table and throwing it into the wall, where it shattered.

"Because the goddamn bookstore was closed!"

Abel clenched his fists and began to weep. I was astonished. I sat on my couch and watched him turn from a frightening teenager into a heartbreaking child. His face and body became if anything more tense, as if his weeping frightened him, too, and the muscles in his face darkened with effort. The scratchy noise of his breathing made him sound as if he were suffocating. I remembered how he had come to me, beaten, wet, and alone.

I cannot say that in the face of his weeping I completely forgot about the screaming that led up to it. But I did *nearly* forget it, or at any rate I put it aside, and I felt sympathy instead. I stood up and approached him, intending, I think, to embrace him. He punched me.

He continued weeping and clenching his fists as if nothing had happened, and I almost doubted that it had. But he had indeed punched me in the stomach, and I stumbled back onto the couch to catch my breath.

"Abel," I said, "I understand that you're upset, but you can't—"

"Fuck you," he screamed. He wiped his eyes with the backs of his hands and moved from tears to shouting. "You send me off to Penley so you can go try to fuck your girlfriend or let the doctor fuck you—"

"Jesus," I said, "shut up!"

"—as if I don't know what you want. Why don't you just lock me in my room if you want me out of the way? Why don't you throw me back in the forest? What am I supposed to do with twenty dollars? You send me to a closed bookstore just to look through some fucking window because I'm so much trouble if I'm sitting here reading a book. You fucking pansy—"

"Shut up," I said, "and go to your room, Abel."

He began laughing hysterically. "I know what to say now," he said, "I know what to say, I know what to say! You must really be a faggot! Tell me, Joseph, is the doctor well endowed?"

Now I was standing with my own fists clenched.

"Tell me, do you let him come in your mouth?"

I stood before him so upset now that I could not move. He reached out and pushed me.

"Does he come in your mouth, Joseph?" he repeated. I opened one fist and slapped Abel hard across the face.

"Go to your room," I said.

CHAPTER SIX

1

I want to say first that I was occasionally struck in my own childhood, and if I doubted myself in the days following Abel's tantrum, it was not in regard to slapping him. If striking a child is ever called for, it was called for then, and there was, moreover, nothing else I could have done.

There was nothing else I could have done, that is, at that moment, once things had progressed as far as they had: once I had taken Abel in, once I had lived with him for three months, once I had let him do as much as he had done. I did question myself for having done any of these things; I remained in the living room that night until long past dark.

I was nervous and frightened, now, to have Abel in my house. I did not know what I would do with him if he behaved like this. It is unfortunately no exaggeration to say that, shocked and terrified by the force of his outburst, I was willing to do almost anything to avoid its repetition. I looked back over everything to do with Abel, but nowhere could I find a missed opportunity. I could not have turned him out the first day. I had not wanted to bring him to the orphanage. The only thing that I could have done better, I thought at the time, would have been to throw him on the doctor's hands as soon as I found him, and that would have seemed an act of cowardice to me.

Finally at about one-thirty in the morning I walked slowly up the stairs to my room, leaving as much distance as possible between myself and Abel's door. I did not sleep well; I woke up at least three times that I remember, and probably more times that I forget. My hands shook when I washed in the morning—I did not know what to expect from my boy when he got up, and I did not look forward to finding out. I told myself that the most likely thing was that he would apologize—as he had for breaking into the store—and that that would be the end of it for the time being. Then in the following calm I could think about what to do. But I did not really believe this.

I entered the kitchen at eight o'clock and began making breakfast. I put water in the kettle and turned on the burner; I took out eggs and bacon and bread; I poured myself a glass of juice. I took the juice with me across the road into the cowshed. I asked Cassandra what she thought of the problem but I did not imagine any answer for her. When I reentered the kitchen I found the lights on and Abel sitting at the table.

"Good morning," he said pleasantly. For a moment what seemed like a flicker of wisdom passed through my mind. Perhaps, I thought, he was only testing me, and precisely because I struck him he will not do it again.

"Good morning," I said, my tone neutral. My flicker of wisdom was wrong, because Abel continued:

"May I have scrambled eggs, please?" he said cheerfully. Whatever the test was I had failed it. It did occur to me to tell Abel that he was welcome to make whatever he wanted, but I did not open my mouth. As always I chose the immediately easier path: it was easier to make the eggs.

While I cooked, Abel made pleasant conversation.

"I think I may go into Penley again this afternoon," he said. "The sign on the bookstore said that it was only closed for the day, and there was one book I saw through the window that I want to get."

I did not answer this, but it softened me slightly. I imagined that he meant the *Brief Study of Bovine Tuberculosis,* and that he meant to buy it for me as an apology. But I quickly realized that this was nothing more than a possibility, and really a faint one, and that whether I could even accept such an apology were it given was difficult to know.

When I had finished cooking I put out the food and sat down across from Abel. He began eating and continued to behave exactly as he might have on any other morning, with a cheerful self-involvement. He did not notice that I was quiet.

"I think the trains run on the hour and half hour," he said. "Do you have any lunch plans? I can eat something in Penley, but if you were planning anything here I could stay."

It took me a few seconds to work up a reply, and he waited patiently.

"I didn't have any special plans," I said at last. "I think that you might as well go earlier and give yourself the time."

"That's a good idea," he said. When he had finished eating he stood up and washed his plates and the frying pan.

"Excuse me," he said, and left the room. It occurred to me then how lucky I had been so far. Here was a child beaten and abandoned and having suffered God only knew what, who had walked all night through the rain to find my door, and only now, after three months, had he broken down for the first time. What is more, there was no sign that it would become an ongoing problem. I decided that it had been very childish of me to take anything Abel said personally, and when he left I told him to have fun. I selflessly cleaned up the lamp.

I ate lunch alone in the house and afterwards I left. The weather was beautiful: there was enough melancholy fall in the air to call for a light jacket, but enough summer, still, that it seemed a terrible waste to stay indoors. I left the house with no destination in mind, thinking vaguely of visiting the doctor, of finding someone at the store to play checkers with, of going to see Diana.

But I felt too restless to play board games, I had just seen the doctor, and I wanted to wait and see if Diana said anything about the flowers I had left her. I walked slowly toward town for a minute until I was struck by inspiration: I still had not taken a walk in the forest.

The day could not have been better for it. The weather was fine, I had already eaten, and Abel was gone on his own volition. There was nothing for me to do but be at peace and enjoy myself.

This is what I did, more or less. I walked into the pine forest excited, at first, at how well circumstances had provided for me. I walked aimlessly as I always did and looked up into the pines. I walked aimlessly and looked into the pines as I always did, but this time there was nothing more to it: I *felt* aimless, and the trees were only trees.

This feeling did not send me home any sooner than usual. I continued walking by force of habit, and in any case the realization that there was nothing in the forest for me only solidified slowly: it was only at the last minute, when the feeling had become too strong and uncomfortable to ignore, that I admitted my failure and turned home.

But the green house seemed just as empty to me, from the outside, as had the green forest, so I crossed the road and entered the cowshed. I scratched my lazy cow on her nose and sat down on the milking stool.

"What do you think, Cassandra?" I said. "Do I need a new purpose in life? Should I buy myself some canvases?"

The cow chewed.

"That's true," I said, "perhaps I should get some paper and charcoal first. Do you think they keep that in the store here?"

I imagined her shrugging as if to say, Go find out. I looked at my watch.

"Maybe I'll go tomorrow," I said. "I think I want to read for an hour or two before dinner."

Cassandra was unimpressed. I scratched her nose again and then locked the shed door behind me. Without thinking I walked past the front door of my green house and around to the back. I stepped up onto the porch and found the back door open. Reflexively I turned to look for someone on the porch, but of course no one was there. I decided that Abel had pulled the door shut behind him without paying attention and the door's stiff tongue had defied the doorway.

"Abel!" I called as I closed the door. I wanted him to come down to the back hallway so that I could lecture him about locking the door. But I instantly changed my mind—I did not want to start another tantrum. It was not such a serious mistake, we were in a small town. No one was waiting to rob us.

But since I had already called his name, I had to make something of it, so I called him again. "Abel, are you home?"

There was no answer. Maybe he had come home and fallen asleep. I realized that I had left that afternoon from the front door, so the back door could have been standing open since Abel left in the morning. I walked upstairs and knocked on his door, and when there was no answer I opened the door and found his room empty.

In my study I found several books left open or lying on their faces on my desk. One of these books—the *Social History of Leprosy in Continental Europe*—had a pencil between its pages, and when I opened the book I found those pages covered with markings. Words and phrases were underlined in some unintelligible pattern, and brief phrases in a cryptic handwriting lined the margins.

The upset books must have shocked me more than I felt, because it was not until I had put them all away (leaving out the *Social History*) that I noticed my microscope. It, too, was standing on my desk, all of its parts and accessories lying haphazardly around it. The eyepiece was dirty.

I managed to spend a full hour cleaning up. I took apart the microscope and cleaned every part. I inspected it reassembled and finally replaced the body and all the parts in the right places in their box and put the box on my highest bookshelf. Then I rummaged in my desk for a good eraser and sat down to restore the social history.

Once I had seen that most of the pencil marks would come off without too much trouble I found some pleasure in the job. By the time I looked up, it was seven o'clock. As I left my study I found my gavel—given to my father by a famous judge and subsequently left to me—on the floor under a chair. I put it on my desk.

I went downstairs to make dinner and begin worrying about Abel. There was nothing at all to do in Bettley at seven o'clock and there was nowhere he could be. I spent a few minutes beside myself until I realized that he must have stayed to eat dinner out in Penley. If he did not get on the train till after dinner, he could not be home before eight or nine.

My lonely dinner was bitter in my mouth. I think it is important to mention that it was a lonely dinner, since I had eaten most of my meals alone for most of my adult life and very few of them had been lonely. Most of my life in the city had been lonely in a certain fundamental sense, but this was a loneliness largely irrelevant to whether I had anyone to talk to at any given time; and the time I had spent in Bettley before Abel arrived had been for the most part wonderful, and I had never felt alone. The pine trees were all around me. But now that I had gotten used to Abel, I had lost my ability to sit by myself.

I went up to my study to read. I read the carefully erased

social history of leprosy. The later it got the less I read and the more I worried, and the front door did not open until long past ten o'clock.

"Where were you?" I asked him. I had run downstairs. "I was worried."

Abel laughed.

"I was in Penley," he said, "at the bookstore."

I looked at my watch demonstratively.

"Is there anything to eat?" he said. I did not answer right away, and he waited patiently.

"You are welcome to help yourself," I said at last, and went back upstairs.

2

I do not know quite how to convey the tone of the following days and weeks. I think that any literal record of what Abel or I said would seem perfectly ordinary; I do not think either of us behaved with any obvious difference. But a definite sourness pervaded everything. Despite my resolution to feel lucky that one tantrum was the worst that had happened, I could not help examining Abel's every remark for a hidden meaning, a hidden sting. I could not speak to him honestly or even comfortably about anything. (I remind you again that I was a childless bachelor and Abel an almost incredibly precocious child: I did not know any way to relate to him except as to an adult.)

One Saturday afternoon Abel and I were both sitting in the living room. He was reading one of the books he had bought himself in Penley, and I was putting on my shoes to go for a walk. I was just standing up when there was a knock at the door.

I found Dr. Ericsson there with a violin case under his arm. "Hello, Joseph," he said. "I haven't seen you for a while."

We shook hands.

"This is excellent timing," I said. "I was just about to take a walk."

"Oh, were you?" he said. "I was coming over to ask if you still play the viola."

"How did you know that I did?"

"I noticed it in your study—do you still?"

"I haven't picked it up—I don't remember for how long. I must be terrible by now."

"Excellent," the doctor said, "so am I."

During this conversation Abel put down his book, put on his shoes, and came to the door. "Are you going to play together now?" he said. I said that we probably were.

"I'm going to take a walk," Abel said. He took the spare key from its hook and put it in his pocket.

"We were only being prophylactically self-deprecating, Abel," the doctor said. "You don't have to leave."

"I'm sure you're very talented," Abel said as he opened the door. "I don't happen to enjoy music."

He shut the door behind him. I was very embarrassed at the boy's behavior and I tried to pretend that it had not happened.

"You need to do something with him," Dr. Ericsson said. "He should start going to school. I don't doubt that he would be bored by the schoolwork, but it would be good for his social development. I can talk to the teacher for you."

"Thank you," I said, "that's a good idea. What do you want to play?"

"Let's go up to the study," the doctor said. "My music is in my case."

Upstairs in my study I produced my dusty viola case and the doctor produced music. My viola has the useful peculiarity of never wandering very far out of tune, so it was quickly ready; Dr. Ericsson propped the music of a duet on the bookcase.

We spent a very pleasant afternoon playing together. After a few minutes of practice I managed to play well enough, and the doctor's skill was good but hardly professional, and so we were perfectly comfortable together. The first piece we played was a sort of canon and variations built on a very simple and beautiful theme. Once we had exhausted the jokes and mistakes we played it through several times, and I, at least, was equally moved by it every time. After the first duet we played another, and then I played the one solo piece that I still remembered, and the doctor taught me one or two simple reels. I enjoyed the contrast between their character and the tone of my instrument.

We were still playing when Abel returned from wherever he had gone, and he came to my study to quietly shut the door. But the doctor saw him there and called him into the room. "Abel," he said, "what do you mean you don't like music? You must mean just string music."

"I don't like any of it," Abel said. "You wouldn't go out of your way to listen to a construction site. Music is just organized noise instead of disorganized noise, and I don't see what difference it makes."

The doctor and I were both incredulous. I don't know

whether Abel meant to defend himself or provoke us, but he reiterated his point. "It's only modulating frequencies," he said.

"So are you," I told him. "Shut the door."

Abel shut the door and left and the doctor and I stood blankly.

"And food is only chemicals," I said, "and a church is only stone."

"Well," the doctor said, "most adolescents grow up."

He looked at his watch and I looked at mine; we put our instruments away.

"I'll walk out with you," I said. The doctor put his case under his arm and we walked into the hallway; I stopped to knock on Abel's door.

"I'm going out for a little while," I said. There was no answer.

I walked the doctor into town and we talked about music. After we parted I went to Diana's house. I still had not heard from her, but by now I did not really care about the flowers, I only wanted to see her. I knocked on her door.

"Joseph," she said. The sleeves of her white blouse were turned up, and she looked as if she had been cleaning.

"Did you get my flowers?" I blurted out.

Diana looked uncomfortable. "Yes," she said, looking away over my shoulder, "thank you."

Then she turned to look directly at me. "Where's my cake?" she said.

This caught me off guard; I stuttered something and looked down at my hands. Diana laughed.

"What kind of cake did you want?" I said.

"Yellow layer cake with coconut filling, white icing, and pink flowers," she said.

"Oh. Do you have a pen?"

I searched in my pockets for a piece of paper.

"I'll remind you," she said. "What are you doing? Do you want to have dinner?"

"No," I said, "I should go home and feed Abel. . . . I just wanted to say hello."

"Oh," Diana said. "All right."

She stuck out her hand and I took it.

"Hello," she said.

"Hello."

After a moment Diana smiled at me and gently closed the door. I stood on her porch.

Finally I made it home to make dinner for Abel. I sat quietly at the table, not really eating, while he expanded at great length his opinions of music. It was a colossal waste of time, a fraud. It made no more sense than astrology, and he could only pity its experts.

By now Abel could so demoralize me that I was incapable of arguing with him; I simply sat there and let him run on. He knew that he was upsetting me and he enjoyed it.

"What about science?" I managed to say.

"Slightly more interesting in practice," he said, "but much duller in principle. It's the difference between counting the bricks in your prison cell walls and inventing complicated lies about them."

I almost cried.

"But what else is there, Abel? What else can you do?" I asked.

"Break out," he answered.

I do not want to be repetitive, but I want to say it once more—he frightened me.

A few days went by in which I was quiet and Abel quietly tortured me. I knew that the doctor would not have let him do it, and I knew that all it took was a simple decision: it was not because the doctor was smarter or stronger than I was—though he may have been—that Abel could not bother him, but because he did not allow it. He did not allow Abel any advantage, and he did not allow himself to care what Abel said. But I could not do it; I was too involved with the child and too insecure; instead I secretly nurtured a growing resentment for the child and even somewhat for the doctor.

One night when Abel had gone to meet someone in Penley—I have no idea who he might have known there—Diana came over. She kissed my cheek quickly and then walked past me into the living room.

"I got a letter from my sister today," she said, almost before I was in the room. "She's getting married."

Diana's sister, Grace, was ten years younger than she was.

"Congratulations," I said.

Diana scratched the nail of her left index finger with her right thumbnail. "Don't you think it's a little young?" she said.

"I don't know," I said. "I imagine if she's got the right person then it's probably the best age."

"Then what does that make me?"

"Oh," I said, "I see."

"Joseph," she said, "I don't know if I can go to the wedding."

"Of course you'll go to the wedding," I said.

"No," she said, standing up, "I really don't know."

I stood up also and found that we were standing quite close together.

"What if you got married first?"

She turned up her clear green eyes to me.

"Who would I marry, Joseph?"

"You could find someone."

We were close enough that I could feel her breath when she spoke.

"Really?" she said.

I looked at the door and stepped back; I cleared my throat.

"When is the wedding?" I asked.

Diana sat down.

"It's in May," she said.

"Oh, you have plenty of time," I said, "eight months! You could almost have children."

Diana laughed.

"It's one thing to get married to show up my sister, Joseph, but I think it would be irresponsible to have children for that reason."

"All right," I said, "then suppose you fall in love this week, get married next week, have a one-week honeymoon, and then consider the matter with your husband for one more week— you'd still have time to show up to the wedding seven months pregnant."

She leaned back in her seat.

"I don't even care so much," she said. "I could just go and

not even think about it; I just know they'll give me a hard time."

"Even at your sister's wedding?"

"Of course," she said, "especially at my sister's wedding. They don't mean to. They'll just ask me what about me, and then they'll be sympathetic, and then they'll be concerned, and they'll never stop talking."

"Shall I go with you and we can pretend to be engaged?"

"No," Diana said, "then we'd have to pretend to plan a wedding, and pretend to get married, and pretend to live together and buy a house and have children."

"Pretend to fight over money," I said.

"Pretend to pay bills and write checks and buy furniture," she said. "We'd have to pretend to be in love."

The room fell still and we avoided looking at each other.

"We could practice," I said.

Diana's eyes lit up with amusement. "Rehearse?" she said. "What do you want to rehearse first, Joseph, buying the furniture or arguing about money?"

"I don't like arguing about money," I said.

"All right," she said, "then what kind of credenza do you want?"

"Never mind."

Diana stood up laughing. "What color shall we paint the bathroom, Joseph?"

"You make your point," I said.

"What about the second bathroom?"

"I hope you feel better," I said. "I appreciate your confiding in me."

We walked toward the door; Diana put one hand on my arm, and with the other she tugged on my shirt. "Joseph," she said, "Joseph, we could go in matching outfits!"

"Good night, Diana," I said firmly. "I'm glad you feel better." She kissed me on the cheek again, and I watched her walk out laughing. After I closed the door behind her I turned around and saw that the house was all dark.

3

Tensions continued to escalate. For example: I made Abel breakfast every morning in September. I did not want to make Abel breakfast any morning in September. But because he consistently awoke at a time that was, it now occurs to me, entirely unnatural for a boy his age, and stationed himself at the kitchen table reading my newspaper, I could not avoid it. He had such a brilliant command of body language and tone of voice that I found myself incapable of arguing with his firm assumption that breakfast would be made and served to him.

A second example: I tried unsuccessfully to discuss starting school with him at least three times. I had not thought much of my chances when the doctor first mentioned it, but as it got harder and harder to have Abel in the house, I came to think that the idea was worth a try. The school year in Bettley began in middle or late September, and it would be better, I thought, for him to start at the beginning. I twice tried to talk about it before school started, and each time he changed the subject so effortlessly and with such calm arrogance that I was entirely defeated.

Then the doctor told me that school had started, and for several days I despaired of getting Abel out of the house at all.

I should mention that one morning Abel read through a calculus book that I happened to have and asked me at lunch whether I had any more.

"I must have at one time," I said. "I did three years of math in college. But I think they would all be together if I still had them."

"It doesn't matter," Abel said.

"Maybe we can get some in Penley," I said. "Did you want a precalculus book, or algebra?"

Abel looked at me contemptuously, as children can sometimes when their ages are mistaken.

"I'm not six years old, Joseph," he said. "This book only has single variable, and you might as well print the answers right next to the exercises. I thought it might get more interesting as it went on."

"Oh," I said. He was not showing off—he was telling the truth.

The point is that he was not missing anything academically by being out of school.

After the first week of school had passed I tried again. "You know, Abel," I said, "we have a fairly good school in Bettley. It's only one room and one teacher, but it's supposed to be—"

"I heard you the first two times you brought it up, Joseph," he answered, "and I think that I made it clear on both of those occasions that I am not interested. Why should I sit in a room for eight hours learning how to spell?"

"No," I said, "that's—but other children—"

"Oh," he said, "I see, you're worried that my future professional success will be hampered by my inadequate training in playing ring-a-levio. Well, Joseph, if that proves to be a problem, I will engage a private tutor."

"No," I said, "I didn't mean—"

"Excuse me," he said, "I'm going to the store."

On this occasion he bought himself six imported shirts in eccentric colors. I had asked him one day to buy some eggs at the store and told him that I had an account. Like a little scientist furnished with a natural clue, he thereupon made an experiment: he bought himself three chocolate bars, two pencils, a notebook, and a necktie. When I was handed my bill at the end of the week, I paid it without remark. I could certainly afford to provide my ward with chocolate bars and pencils, and every young man should have a necktie.

I did resolve to discuss with him an appropriate budget or allowance, but I could not quite bring it up. He therefore increased his purchases the following week, and continued doing so, and I became embarrassed to say anything. I anticipated his being ashamed and was preemptively embarrassed for him, and for my own part I felt guilty at not having said anything immediately. By the end of September the boy had more clothing than I did and, by means of the shopkeeper's relationship with the bookstore in Penley, a small library.

One day in the middle of the month Diana came over to the green house to borrow a book. (I think it was a cookbook; I do not read cookbooks, although I happen to own some, so I cannot remember what it was.) When we walked into the living room, talking about the fall weather, Abel looked up from his book as if disturbed in his own study and interrupted me.

"What can I do for you?" he said to Diana. He stared at her intensely as he said this, and she was startled and then transfixed—it took her several seconds to reply.

"I came to borrow a book from Joseph," she said.

"Oh," Abel said carelessly, "can you read?"

Diana opened her mouth and did not speak; I looked back and forth between them, but I could say nothing either. Finally I asked Diana to sit down and I walked upstairs to my study. In my study I found the cookbook, an ink stain on my desk, and, in the wastepaper basket, a piece of chewing gum wrapped in the corner of page 101 of the *Concise Dictionary of Epidemiology.*

As I came back down the stairs I heard Abel speaking rapidly in a low voice; I did not hear Diana; I thought I heard my name. Abel stopped talking abruptly as I entered the room and opened his book again. Diana thanked me for the cookbook and left immediately.

"What did you say to her?" I demanded.

Abel did not look up from his book. "I was only making conversation," he said.

I took a deep breath, clenched my fists, and left the room.

A fourth example: I had to pack away my record player. I occasionally liked to listen to one of Bach's masses in the evening after dark. But Abel explained to me, apologetically at first and later patiently and indulgently, that he found it distracting to hear music through the wall: in the face of whatever he was trying to do, he said, he found himself compelled to imagine the full sound of the music. I invited him to join me in my study, where he could hear the full sound, but of course he did not like music.

I bought myself a pair of earphones but eventually I packed

these, too, away with the record player. I had difficulty in the abstract believing that enough sound could leak between the earphones and my ears for Abel to hear through the wall, but whenever I put the earphones on and turned on the machine he would appear almost instantaneously with a soft knock on the door. The soft knock quickly turned into a hostile banging. It occurs to me now that what he heard was probably only the clicking of the turntable.

My fifth example: his tantrums. He had several tantrums in the month of September. None was as long or as terrible as the first one. In fact I would not even think to call them tantrums if I had not seen the first one. We would be having what was, for the period, a pleasant conversation and then he would suddenly break: he would shout something irrelevant or unreasonable or begin punching the wall. Then just as suddenly he would stop, and if I said anything about it he would pretend to have—or actually have—no idea what I meant, and would make a cool comment about *my* strange behavior.

I think the truth is that he was only partially aware of his own actions. During one of these momentary fits he picked up a bowl from the table and threw it across the room; it shattered against the wall, and the pieces fell to the floor. We both stood for a moment unmoving, I laboriously deciding what to do and he still in the grip of whatever possessed him. Then, like the turning of a switch, he regained his self-control. He looked down at the broken bowl and smiled an offensive smile. "What happened to the bowl?" he said.

I was not sure at the time whether he was gloating at my impotence or honestly implying that I had broken the bowl myself. I would say now that it was something between the two. In the event I picked up the pieces as Abel sat down at the table and continued explaining to me his feelings about international cooperation.

In another momentary fit he tore all the pages out of a book. Again I did nothing, but not this time because I did not know what to do. I did nothing because the only thing I really wanted to do was throttle him dead. When the fit passed he cleaned up after himself but he did not apologize. He picked up the book's hard cover and gathered its torn pages and took them outside to the garbage can. He came back in, walked up to his room, and slammed the door.

But this slammed door, I want to say, was the only suggestion I can remember that his fits had any emotional effect on him. The slammed door in fact made me sympathetic despite my brief murderousness and I walked up to talk to him. I knocked gently on his door, and he told me calmly to come in.

"Abel," I began softly. Then I noticed that he was lazily leaning back in his armchair reading a mathematics textbook. He did not look upset. I sat down on his bed and decided to continue anyway.

"You've been here for a few months," I said, "and I realize that we've never talked about your feelings."

"Are you working up to offering me a massage, Joseph?" he said. I shut my eyes for a moment and gathered my self-control.

"I'm phrasing it badly," I said, forcing myself to smile. "I meant, Abel, that I don't really know whether you're happy or at peace, and I feel remiss in not having asked. I don't want to make you upset now, but I can't help thinking that you may

have experienced things that would leave you still angry or
unhappy about them or in general."

I had not looked at him as I said this, concentrating as I was
on careful diction, but now I looked up and saw that he was
waiting for me to finish with a slight smile on his face.

"Perhaps," I said, "you might like someone qualified to
speak to."

"I'm sorry," he said. "I see that you were leading up to having the doctor give me a massage."

He laughed a small laugh and turned his attention back to
his book. I walked out.

That day I had been invited to the doctor's house for dinner.
I left Abel with food prepared and walked into town around
seven o'clock. I got as far as knocking on the doctor's door with
the intention of discussing Abel with him. But once he opened
the door and invited me in, and I said hello to Lucy, the idea
dropped from my mind.

Lucy is a woman whose calm stability provides her with
inexhaustible friendliness, and she is, moreover, the sort of person who believes so strongly that all things work out for the best
that when in her presence it is hard to disagree. For two and a
half hours the three of us talked about art and music and I forgot that I did not live alone. But then, inevitably, I left.

I did not realize that I had forgotten my key until I was at my
front door. I knocked. I knocked again. I walked around to the
back and knocked on that door and then knocked on it again. I
stood outside the back and yelled up toward Abel's window on
the second floor. I returned to the front and began banging on
the door, growing angrier with each blow.

I felt convinced that Abel was sitting in the living room listening to me bang, and it made me furious. I quickly lost the voice for shouting but I continued banging with both hands for fifteen or twenty minutes. Then I felt someone watching me and I stopped.

"What's the matter?"

It was Abel speaking from behind me. I turned around.

"Why are you making so much noise?" he said. He was wearing a bathrobe and slippers. It was a cool night but he looked comfortable; he could not have been outside for very long.

"Where were you?" I demanded. Abel approached the door before speaking.

"I noticed that you had forgotten your key," he said, "and I thought I would take it to you at the doctor's. I guess we missed each other."

His speech was mild and malicious and clearly lying.

"There's only one path between the doctor's house and this house," I said.

"I went out the back door and cut through the forest," he said. "I must have just missed you."

He unlocked the door and entered and I caught the door as it swung shut. I knew that he was lying, but his tone was so dryly sincere that I could not say anything about it. My key was hanging in the front hall. I put it into my pocket and went up to bed.

CHAPTER SEVEN

1

In the morning I resolved not to make breakfast, whatever his body language, but he preempted me: he was up and frying eggs when I walked into the kitchen.

"Sit down, Joseph," he said, "you make me nervous."

He was by now very adept at tying my motivations in knots: I had been about to sit down when he said this, but then I did not want to seem to obey him, but then I thought that changing my course of action for his sake was no different from obeying him. Finally I did sit down.

"Are you a Jew, Joseph?" he said.

"What?"

Abel paused to put a greasy plate in front of me and drop two burnt fried eggs on it. He did not provide a fork.

"I was wondering if you were a Jew," he said. "Your middle name is Seligman."

"Thank you," I said, standing up to get a fork, "I am aware of my middle name."

"Are you avoiding the question?" he said. He put two perfectly cooked eggs onto his own plate and sat down. As I returned to the table with a fork in my hand, he took it from me, and I silently turned to get another.

"Are you ashamed of your Hebrew blood, Joseph?" he said.

"I'm not ashamed of anything," I said. I sat down in front of my burnt breakfast angry and defeated. "My mother was Jewish but I was baptized."

"Thank God," Abel said. "That must be why you don't have horns."

As he said this, I was standing up to throw away my burnt eggs: I sat down.

"What are you talking about?"

Abel smiled at me.

"As far as you know," he said, "I've never met a Jew. How do I know whether they really have horns?"

I did not answer this. I refused to play along. I stood up again.

"Although," he said, "according to the law, I believe, it's being born of a Jewess that makes you a Jew."

"*Jewess,*" I said through my teeth, now facing the sink, "is not a word."

"All right," he said magnanimously, "I'll rephrase what I said. It's being squeezed out by a dank, inbred Jew bitch that makes you a Jew because the kink passes right from her cunt to your head. How do you feel about that phrasing? I suppose there's plenty of Christian blood up here for Passover, but I don't know where you find the crackers or the chicken fat."

I clutched the edge of the sink with trembling hands and shouted the worst possible answer.

"I told you I was baptized!"

Abel chuckled—he had won.

"There's nothing to be ashamed of," he said, and I left the room.

I stamped up to my study, humiliated and ashamed, and tried to read a book. I could barely see the titles on the spines, but I could see, after a moment, that half of my books were on the shelves upside down.

Abel entered. "Diana's also half kinky, isn't she," he said. "Does she smell like a kike?"

I put my hands to my temples.

"You know what I mean," Abel said. Then he laughed and changed the subject before I could respond.

"Listen," he said, "since I made breakfast I'm going to let you wash the dishes. I left them in the sink. You shouldn't leave the pan too long or else the eggs will stick."

I clutched at the spine of a book. Abel sat down in the armchair and crossed his legs.

"I wonder what your children would be," he said. "Would they be all white, all kike, or just plain colored?"

I pulled a book from the shelf.

"No one likes a mulatto, Joseph," he said, "black or otherwise. You should think about that if you ever figure out how to fuck her."

I raised my arm to throw my book at him; I had shut my eyes but I could aim by sound. But before I could throw mine, I was hit in the chest by his. He had thrown it like a discus and it knocked the wind out of me. I collapsed back into my chair and I looked down at the floor.

My Bible had fallen onto open pages; they were all bent and dirty.

"That's funny," Abel said as he stood up. "The Bible was the first book at hand. It's quite the little allegory, isn't it, Joseph? I feel like Saint Paul."

As he walked out of the room he bellowed in a clownish voice that he found very amusing. "Saul, Saul!" he bellowed. "Why persecutest thou me?"

I slammed shut the door of my study and turned the lock. I do not know what Abel did for the rest of the day because, to avoid him, I did not leave my study. But by dinnertime I was hungry and restless, so I unlocked the door to go down to the kitchen.

Abel's door was open and he must have been waiting for me. As soon as I entered the hallway he jumped out of his room and he followed me down the stairs. "What's for dinner, Joey?" he said.

"I don't know."

"I apologize for baiting you about your Judaism," he said. He was walking only a couple of inches behind me, and the muscles of my back were knotting under his eyes. "I didn't think that you would be so sensitive about it."

I declined to answer this.

Once we got into the kitchen he sat down at the table. "But I probably would be, too," he went on, "especially if I were a half-breed."

"Do you expect to eat dinner?" I asked.

"Do you expect to make it?"

"If you expect to eat dinner," I said, my heart racing and my hands trembling, "you should be quiet."

"Oh!" Abel said. It was obvious how nervous I was. "Oh, dear!" he said. "Look who's asserting himself!"

"I'm not joking, Abel," I said.

"Oh, oh, certainly not. Of course not. I take you seriously, Joey, don't worry. I will obey."

Abel made a great production of straightening his chair, straightening his back, and sitting with his mouth tightly closed and his hands in his lap. I moved around the kitchen assembling ingredients with difficulty. It was hard to concentrate on what I was doing; I felt like a mouse in a room with a cat. All my attention was drawn to Abel whether I was looking at him or not; he remained the center of the room wherever I moved.

"Forgive me breaking the silence, Josephus," Abel said, "but I ought to tell you that I don't eat chicken."

I had just begun breading chicken cutlets. The right thing to do would have been to ignore him, or, failing that, to tell him that if he did not eat chicken he would be out of luck that night. I could also have asked him since when, since I knew that he was lying. But at the time, still a good person, so to speak, I made an angry but silent show of throwing away the chicken and taking out two steaks.

Abel spoke again once I had begun to cook them. "Forgive me again, Josephine," he said, "but all good chefs agree that steak should be served rare."

I took his steak off the fire and put it in front of him; it was still bloody, but he did not care. He had finished eating it by the time I sat down with my own.

"I don't want any potatoes," he said, and he stood up and left the room.

I knew that I was allowing him to behave badly, and even in a sense encouraging it, but I could not stop.

As the month continued I began spending more and more of every day out of the house. I took some long walks through the forest, but the weather was too cold to do this often. I would go to the store to play checkers with retired old men. But I have little facility for board games even when I can concentrate, and I had no conversation to make, and I soon saw that I was not entirely welcome. Sometimes I gathered a few books, put on an extra layer of clothing, and went to spend the day in the cowshed. This last trick only worked until Abel found me.

"Josephus!" he said when he saw me. "What are you doing in here? Reading to the cow?"

"What are *you* doing?" I answered. "Were you coming to milk her?"

"Don't be disgusting," he said. "I'm bored to death here."

"Why don't you go to Penley?"

"Penley is only slightly less boring," he said.

"Or to school?" I asked. Abel did not answer: he was walking around the small shed, peering into corners and looking under things.

"What are you looking for?"

"Does this door lock?" he said.

"It locks from the outside."

He nodded his head and left. I turned back to my book with relief, but only for a moment. Shortly I realized what he had just asked me, and I leaped up, dropping my book and almost toppling a kerosene lamp, to try the door. It swung open easily and I stumbled out into the cold air. Abel was gone.

The next day I went to Penley myself. I had not been there for years. I got up well before dawn and snuck out of the house just as the sky was lightening. I had to wait at the station for half an hour for the first train, and there were only two or three other passengers on it.

I enjoyed myself in Penley. I went to the bookstore, I ate in restaurants, I inspected their small museum. There was even a café to sit in and read the newspaper in the late afternoon. But I only enjoyed myself up to a point: the pleasure descended in a steady curve through the day, reaching bottom as I returned to the train station.

There was a small hotel in Penley, and it did occur to me to stay there, but I knew that it would not be right. It would not be right to leave Abel alone, and it would also, I thought, be unwise to leave my house alone with him; then, too, I had begun to have a faint idea that I did not want to be chased out of my house.

It was long past dark by the time I walked into the green house.

"There are dishes in the sink," Abel said as I walked by. I went up to my room and went to sleep. I spent the rest of the week visiting Penley.

2

On the last day of this week I became suddenly tired of the town in the middle of the afternoon and I decided to go home for dinner. The sun was just setting as I walked quickly through Bettley toward my home. As I rounded the turn in the road I caught sight of someone at my door: it was Diana.

"Hello," I said, and she turned, and I said, "I'm glad to see you."

"Where were you?" she asked me.

"I spent the day in Penley," I said. "I'm just getting back."

I took out my key and opened the door. "Will you come in?" I said.

Diana's eyes darted into the living room before she answered. "All right," she said, and she followed me in.

"Sit down," I told her, and she did. She put down the book she had borrowed from me on the coffee table.

"Will you stay for dinner? I was just going to make something."

"Where's Abel?" she asked.

"I don't know."

I began making dinner and Diana sat silently in the living room. After a few minutes Abel came walking down the stairs. When he saw me in the kitchen and Diana in the living room, he stopped in his tracks and smiled. It is an old-fashioned expression, but I think it is most accurate to say that he smiled like a fox in a chicken coop. He ran his fingers through his shining dark hair.

"Well," he said, "look at this. Cooking dinner for your lady friend?"

"She hasn't said yet whether she's staying."

"I'd like to stay, Joseph," Diana said.

Abel stepped forward. "Will I be intruding?" he said. I was chopping carrots on the counter, and I did not see the predatory look that he must have given Diana.

"Not exceptionally," I said.

Abel walked into the living room and sat down. I chopped quietly so that I could hear him speaking, but I only caught pieces; he made several remarks before I heard anything.

"Because your name, Diana," I heard Abel say, "comes from an infelicitous combination of kike and mick just like you yourself come from an infelicitous combination of cunt and dick."

I turned away from what I was doing and leaned over the counter nearer the living room. "What did you just say, Abel?" I demanded. Diana was sitting back stunned, mouth open, eyes wide.

"I was just telling your friend Diana Green Greene," he said, "that her name fits her perfectly. Would you like us to come stand around you in the kitchen where you'll be able to hear us better?"

Abel's eyes were gloating and his cheeks were red.

"No," I said, "stay where you are."

I made a point now of chopping loudly, but I only carried this on for a few moments. My curiosity won out over my dignity and I began working quietly and straining my ears again.

"I'm sorry," I heard Abel say, "of course I meant felicitous. Measuring a woman by her brain is like measuring a man by his cooking. Are you sure, Josephus," he called out, "that you wouldn't like to come sit down?"

I began chopping loudly again and straining my ears all the more as I ostentatiously paid them no attention. In any case they seemed to stop talking; they only sat on their couches and looked at each other.

I have no excuse for allowing this to go on, but as an explanation, at least, I will say that even then I put more faith in Abel's youth than in his danger. When Abel was present, moreover, my struggle with him absorbed me entirely, and though it is incredible even to me now, the fact is that for most of this dinner Diana's position simply did not occur to me.

Abel smirked and pulled out Diana's chair for her, and she accepted the gesture nervously. She was the first one to speak. "What have you been reading recently, Joseph?" she asked me.

"I just read *The Razor's Edge*," I began.

Abel interrupted me. "He's just been reading about death and decay like he always does," he said. His voice was strong and filled the room. "What about you, Diana? You never answered my question the other day. Can you read? If so, what do you read?"

Diana looked at her plate; she looked up at me through her eyelashes.

"I was rereading *Anne of Green Gables* last night," she said.

"How charming," Abel said.

"What do you read, Abel?" Diana said.

"Novels about sensitive young girls with red hair," he said. "Let me ask you a question—are you hoping that the ending will be better this time?"

Diana did not answer.

"What was the name of that novel, Josephus," Abel said,

"about the English peer who discovers that his mother is actually a Jewish washerwoman that his father raped in the laundry?"

"Let me ask you one, Abel," I said.

"I can't remember the title, but I think Diana would enjoy it."

"Let me ask you one, Abel."

"I think it would resonate with her. Tell me something, Diana, do you always chew your hair during dinner? I think Joseph would serve you more meat if you asked him to."

"Can you tell me something, Abel?" Diana said. "Are you always this obnoxious?"

Abel laughed artificially as if delighted. "Well played, Diana Greene! You almost made me cry. Look at me, Josephus, my hands are shaking!"

"Let me ask you a question, Abel," I said. "Have you read Chaloner's *Against Mencius*? It's all about the case of the child falling into a well and why he should be left to drown."

"I'm more interested in Legalism, Josephine," Abel said, easily dismissing me and my comment both. "Let me ask you, Diana," he said, "if you read *Anne of Green Gables* when you're a grown-up, is it racier?"

"Abel," I said.

"Does Matthew take Anne out to the barn and teach her the facts of life?"

"*Abel,*" I said.

He held up a hand to forestall me. "You're right, Josephus," he said seriously. "I'm sorry, Diana, I'm being very obnoxious."

Diana shrugged but she did not look up.

"I don't mean to offend you," Abel said. "I just don't know how to tell you how I feel."

Diana looked up alarmed. "How you feel?" she said.

"I never know what to say and the words all come out wrong," he said.

"You might try thinking before you speak," Diana muttered.

"Oh," he said breezily, "I never think. Thinking is quite overrated."

"What are you talking about?" she demanded.

"I don't ever think," Abel said. I stood up and cleared my dishes away. Abel waited to continue until I was out of sight, but he and I both knew that I would remain in earshot. "I only act."

Diana stared at him.

"I only think as a surrogate for action when action is impossible," he went on. "But I never think about what I'm doing."

"That's ridiculous, Abel," Diana said, "you have to think about what to do sometimes."

"Not at all," Abel said. "You would be much happier if you gave in to your impulses." He leaned forward as he said this and very slightly leered; I leaned forward and clutched the kitchen counter. "This reminds me of a book you should read," he continued. "You don't mind if I make you a reading list?"

Diana began chewing her hair again.

"'Sephus!" he called out. "Do you have *The Book of Five Rings* in the house?"

This, finally, was too much for me, and I stormed out of the kitchen. "Are you kidding me?" I shouted. "You think you're Musashi because you break into general stores and piss on the floor?"

Abel leaned back in his chair and smiled as if to mean that

this outburst was exactly what he had been trying to effect. "I am," he said, "if I break into shops without remorse."

Abel rested his right hand on his table knife and I closed my hand into a fist.

"There is a difference," I said, "my little samurai, between a stoic lack of regret and a sociopathic lack of remorse. In fact, I would go further and say that the two are actually opposite."

"Nevertheless, Joseph," Abel said, "you surprise me. You are casting my past up to me in a very unchristian manner."

"By birth," I answered him, "I am a Jew."

Abel grinned hatefully. "Good," he said, "I'm so glad you're finally accepting the fact that one baptism doesn't wash the stink off."

I stepped forward and Abel began to close his fingers around his knife. In the corner of my eye I saw that Diana had gone paper white. I stepped back.

"Let me walk you home, Diana," I said. "Diana, let me walk you home."

Diana stood up, walked to the door, and put on her coat.

While she stood there I walked at Abel and he let go the knife. "Clear the table before I get back," I said.

Leaving him there I herded Diana through the doorway and shut the door behind me. The night was black and cold.

I started to speak and then Diana slipped her hand into my hand. We walked this way back to her door. There I took the key from her hand and turned the lock. I slipped the key into her pocket. As we stood before her door in the cold silence I touched my hand to the small of her back and the stars were bright above us. Her eyes were green and fragile.

"I'm sorry, Diana," I began; I meant to go on and make a better apology, but I interrupted myself by kissing her. Her lips were cool; she kissed me back.

"I don't want you to go back," she said.

"It's my house," I answered her. She squeezed my hand and I left her.

When I returned to the green house the table was not cleared, but Abel had not wasted his time: every plate, glass, and serving dish was turned over, and the knives all pointed down.

3

"I promise you, Michael," I said to the doctor, "I am beginning to feel sympathy for Cain the son of Adam."

I had gone to the doctor's office late the following afternoon to ask for his advice.

"I began thinking last night that it would be an act of virtue for someone to kill the boy—it would be a virtuous murder that took him out of the world."

"Joseph," the doctor said, "I don't believe you. You're only upset. Remember when we were discussing the translation of the commandments?" He laughed to try to lighten my mood. "We agreed that murder was wrong."

"God damn it," I shouted, and I banged the table, "that's *why* it would be virtuous. It would be an act of moral self-sacrifice for everyone else's good."

"Joseph," he said, speaking gravely now, "listen to me. I agree with you that this child is extraordinarily obnoxious. He is also extremely intelligent and clearly knows how to bother people. But listen to me, Joseph, it is not appropriate to talk about murdering him."

"Maybe not yet," I said. "But, Michael, it keeps getting worse, and I don't know where it will end. Where will it end?"

"Joe," he said, "with great respect I want to say to you that you've lived alone for a long time, and it's difficult to get used—"

"I was very happy with him for months," I said. "Listen to *me*. It is not in my normal character to think this way about people. I've spent most of my life at the opposite extreme. I think that I deserve the benefit of the doubt. If I am having homicidal thoughts, then my young boarder is provoking them. *Listen* to me. You didn't see him with Diana last night. If I hadn't been there he might have done anything to her. I can't be there all the time! Michael—"

"You need to send him—"

"No!" I shouted, "I am not giving up yet."

The doctor looked at his fingernails.

"Would you like me to try speaking to the boy?" he said.

"Please."

I closed my eyes and took another deep breath before I stood up. The doctor walked me graciously to my blue-green house. In the dining room the dishes remained on the table upside down, and the tablecloth was sticky with food: I had not cleaned up the mess and neither had Abel.

As soon as we walked in I sat down on the couch and clenched my fists; Dr. Ericsson looked at me, and at the table, with concern. "I'll just go up and find him," he said.

The doctor told me afterwards that it was that day that he

decided to make a detailed account of Abel's case. When he got home that evening he sat down and wrote out everything that he and the boy had said to each other. Later he added what he remembered of previous exchanges. Once everything had long since been ended, but before I began writing this, he showed me his notes; I have referred to them generally, and in the case of the following conversation, for the obvious reason that I was not there, I have relied on them entirely.

Dr. Ericsson walked up the stairs to the second floor and found Abel's door. When he knocked, Abel called out, "What do you want, Josephus?" The doctor did not answer but opened the door and entered.

"I didn't say 'come in,'" Abel said. He was standing at the window with his back to the door. "Are you trying to catch me naked?"

Then Abel turned around and saw who it was.

"Oh," he said, "forgive me. You're a different old faggot entirely. What do you want?"

"I want your tender love," Dr. Ericsson said; this disarmed Abel entirely.

"What?" he shouted.

"I want to talk to you, little boy," the doctor said. "Sit down on the bed."

Abel did not move, so the tall doctor approached him, stretched one hand out over his face, and pushed him down on the bed. He himself sat on a round armchair that Abel had stolen from my study.

"I want to ask you a question, Abel," the doctor said. "Why are you so obnoxious here?"

Abel took the question as proof of his strong position and came alive again. He laughed contemptuously. "Joseph complained to you about me?" he said.

"On the contrary," the doctor answered, "he confided in me his intention to strangle you to death, and I don't like performing autopsies on children. There isn't enough room to move the scalpel."

"I don't believe that," Abel said. "Does he cry when you fuck him too hard?"

The doctor did not answer this. Instead he sat back in his chair and observed Abel serenely—so Abel continued.

"What a pathetic inversion of the Greek ideal," Abel said, "that he's your little boy instead of the pederast raping you at a dinner party. Is there money exchanged? Does he like to be whipped?"

"The usual interpretation of remarks like that, Abel," the doctor said, "is that they represent a desperate attempt to repress one's own homosexuality. But no one's judging you here, Abel, you can be open with your feelings."

"Really?" Abel said. "Then why don't you come over here and suck my dick?"

The doctor smiled.

"On the other hand," he said, "in the case of a boy of your intelligence and obvious inexperience, I imagine that they are more likely to represent general concerns over the adequacy of your sexuality rather than its mode. It's really too bad that you should be so damaged before you're even old enough to shake hands with a girl."

"I worry about nothing."

"Have it your way," the doctor said. "I presume that that's only overcompensating braggadocio, but maybe it's true. If so you must be much less intelligent than I thought you were."

"You're nothing but a talking monkey," Abel said.

"Is that right?"

"You're a fucking circus act," Abel said. "Come see the diagnosing nigger, twenty-five cents. The people in this town must be harder up than they look if they let you put your black hands on them."

"Do you want me to put my black hands on you, little boy? It just isn't worth my time. Anyway, I want to help you."

"You want to help me get my dick sucked," Abel said. "Why don't you get the fuck out of my room and go back to your voodoo dolls."

The doctor laughed.

"You're not much bigger than a voodoo doll yourself, Abel," he said. "Maybe someone should stick some pins in you. But why don't you shut up for a minute? I'm trying to tell you something."

Abel stood up from the bed.

"Listen to me," he said. The doctor meanwhile calmly bent down and untied his left shoe. He removed the shoe while Abel, distracted, watched him silently. The doctor crossed his leg, looked at his unshod foot, and then looked at Abel.

"Sit still for a minute, kid," he said, and Abel sat down. "You just a moment ago suggested that I get out of your room. But it is not your room. This room along with the rest of the house belongs to Joseph. He has graciously taken you in and paid for, among other things, that ridiculous purple shirt you're wearing.

Do you think you're Caesar? I want you to explain something to me. You've found here a rich and generous man without a family of his own who showed himself willing to provide for you indefinitely—why are you trying to make him throw you out?"

Abel narrowed his eyes and stared at the doctor belligerently.

"I don't doubt," the doctor said, "that you have very grave insecurities and problems of self-worth, that for whatever reason you know nothing but betrayal and abuse. For that you have my sincere compassion. But you must deal with the reality: Joseph is not your father, and his obligation to you only goes so far. There is only so much you can do to him before you drive yourself and your purple shirt out into the rain."

Abel narrowed his eyes still further and stood up from the bed.

"I want you to take it as a compliment, Abel," the doctor said, "to your intelligence, and as an indication of my deep concern for you, that I have spoken to you so frankly. I want to help you."

Abel opened his mouth, just slightly, to speak, and his voice sounded as if it began in the marrow of his pelvis and was painfully being drawn out bit by bit.

"You goddamn dancing bush nigger faggot," Abel said. "I'm almost sorry for you. You think that a degree from some tropical fly-by-night phony fucking medical school will cover your nigger stink, but dancing like a man and talking like a man doesn't make you one because your color goes all the way to the bottom. Black isn't as black does, it is what it is, and I don't care how many cocks you sucked getting up. Some broken ostensibly white kike motherfucker can let a monkey suck his dick but it sure as fucking hell doesn't make the monkey a human being."

Dr. Ericsson with perfect equanimity raised his eyebrows to inquire whether Abel had finished speaking.

"That you require therapy," the doctor said, "is without question; my only question is whether we would be well advised to begin medicating you immediately."

Abel took one step closer to the doctor.

"You shit-eating jungle bunny," he said. "You have to leave your house and come bully a child to make yourself feel big? You must have the smallest dick on the planet. I bet your wife's got a bigger dick than you. She probably fucks you like a dyke. And you come talk to me? If I were a nigger doctor I'd live with white people too, but it wouldn't be because I felt good about myself. I would know my fucking place. And if your place is at the bottom of this shitheap of a town then you must be a god-damned scientific miracle because it makes you less than fucking nothing. Jesus Christ, if I were a black faggot I would stay away from little boys if I didn't want to get myself lynched."

The doctor notes that it was the purity of Abel's expression during this particular paragraph of abuse that convinced him that nothing could be done with him. He realized that he was hearing not an outburst of fear or defiance so much as an expression of the boy's character on its most fundamental level, far beneath the polite young man and the urbane dinner guest.

"You need a little fine-tuning of your racist invective, little boy," the doctor said. "It's not entirely convincing—but I'm sure you'll figure it out. But its literary merit notwithstanding, you are acting out one of the better allegories of racism that I've ever seen. There you are, little white boy trying to infantilize me because you yourself have never had to grow up. . . . Little white man and big black devil—anyway, that's all, please do continue."

Abel's arms were bent by his sides now as if he were ready to leap onto the doctor, and his fingers were curled into claws.

"I hope your big fat head ripped open your mother's cunt up to her fucking breasts," Abel said. "I hope that she bled to death, whatever black gutter bitch sow dropped you out between rags and the scum on her thighs, with johns coming all in her face, the fucking whore."

Abel was standing directly in front of the doctor now, snarling and spitting; but when the doctor stood up, his size and his confidence were sufficient to frighten Abel into several backward steps, as the doctor followed, and finally into sitting down on his bed.

"Are you talking about my mother?" Dr. Ericsson said, looking down over the boy on the bed. "Are you trying to get me to hit you, little boy?"

Abel looked up, clearly frightened, but whether from bravery or from sheer desperate evil, he remained unmoving and angry. Dr. Ericsson reached out one strong arm and brought one great hand to Abel's face: he held the tip of his index finger with his thumb and then he flicked Abel lightly across the nose.

"Beep," the doctor said.

For a moment Abel was stunned; then he was hysterically furious. He threw himself at the doctor, biting and scratching while with his right hand reaching for the dirty clasp knife he still kept in his pocket. The doctor calmly raised his right hand

and clapped Abel on the side of the face, knocking him off the bed and into the wall.

The doctor closed the door behind him.

"Take him to the orphanage," he told me. "In the meantime, put a lock on his door."

CHAPTER EIGHT

1

Less happened after the doctor left than you might expect. Of course I did not know what had gone on between him and Abel, and I was not waiting for any special tantrum. The only active unpleasantness was when Abel came downstairs to call me a miserable pansy faggot for getting the doctor to do something that I did not hear because I hit him in the face. He went back upstairs and that was for all intents and purposes the end of the day.

The next two or three days passed with ominous but quiet bitterness. I could almost feel in the air some violence ready to fall out, but for the time being it did not. I prepared meals and Abel ate; we did not speak. I spent the time in my study, doing nothing really but waiting, and I imagine that Abel did the same in his room.

The doctor had advised me to send Abel to the orphanage, but I did not even consider it. At this point the boy was too much a part of my life: if I sent him away without settling anything, I thought, I would remain for the rest of my life in the same terrible state that I felt myself in then. But I did follow the other part of the doctor's advice: I went out to buy a lock for Abel's door.

Perhaps because the long silence at home made me desperate for company I was, for once, able to have a long and comfortable conversation with the shopkeeper and the other men that stayed around the store; I even played a few games of checkers. I was given a cup of tea. In the end I was at the store for nearly two hours and it was fully dark out when I left.

I found my front door open and I went upstairs to see if Abel was home. I heard a noise from his room that sounded like crying but did not sound like Abel; I knocked sharply on the door and it swung open.

Diana was there, lying prone on Abel's bed, her white shirt ripped open and her skirt thrown up. Her white skin shone like fire. Diana sobbed as Abel held her wrists in one hand and, with the other, raped her with the handle of my gavel.

I was across the room in an instant. I pushed Abel aside with a hand on his throat, then seized the gavel and struck him across the face with it. When he stumbled but did not fall, I kicked him in the stomach, and this put him down in the corner struggling for breath. While this happened Diana pulled in her legs and arms and began crying more fiercely. After a moment she turned over on her back.

I looked at Diana, not seeing her face or her tears or her exposed body discretely but only a glowing yellow-tinged whiteness. But her nakedness must have somehow entered my mind because the indistinct color I saw was shot through with it; I felt a tingling in my mouth and my arms began to tremble. But then in the corner Abel shifted his weight and caught my eye, and I turned away from the moon to look at ashes.

Glad that I had put on boots that morning I turned to kick the boy in the ribs. Having caught his breath he had cautiously remained sitting where I had thrown him; now he rolled and coughed until I reached down and took his ear to pull him to his feet. I think that Diana watched me as I pulled him out of the room.

I ran down the steps dragging Abel stumbling behind me. I kept my fist tightly around his ear and my arm too low for him to stand up straight. I brought him across the ground floor to the basement door. I let go of him to open the door; he stood his ground and smirked at me, so I pushed him down the stairs.

I followed him down to make sure that he had not broken his neck, and before I got to the bottom I saw him, face bruised and bloody, stand up and dart across the room to hide behind some boxes. There was no light but what came from the doorway at the top of the stairs and I lost sight of him.

My toolbox was right by the stairs. I took out a hand drill and a screwdriver, closed the box, walked up the stairs, and shut the door behind me. The basement door did not lock, but I expected Abel to remain hiding for some time. I went up to the second floor to Abel's door; the padlock sat where I had dropped it on the floor. I picked it up and mounted it on the wall. Then I opened the door and went in.

Diana lay still on Abel's bed, on her back, her shirt still open and her hands covering her face. As I walked toward her, the smell and the color of her body, the strength of the muscle and the softness of the fat, the glistening of sweat and the grace of her neck, the tips of her breasts and the points of her elbows, everything of her entered into me and drove out everything of myself. Time stopped, and as I leaned over her and moved her hands from her face I was possessed. Diana looked at me with open green eyes, I could see down through them as if into wells, and I opened my mouth and I kissed her. Her tongue was sweet and her teeth were cool.

2

In the morning I awoke before her. It was far past dawn and the room was full of light. Even the light switches and the door handles seemed to glow. Diana's brown hair shone almost gold, and the sharper lines of her face were still softened by sleep; she looked like a vision, but I could hear her breath, regular and very deep. Taking care not to wake her, I got out of bed and dressed, and then I crept downstairs to the kitchen.

I found Abel sitting at the table, reading the newspaper with trembling hands. He had washed his face but it was still swollen and cut in several places. He looked up at me nervously.

"Good morning," I whispered, "shhh."

He continued to read nervously while I made breakfast. I fried eggs and bacon and potatoes and made toast. I made tea. I put down one meal in front of the boy, and I put the other on a tray to bring upstairs; I was not hungry.

I sat in my bedroom with the tray on my lap watching Diana sleep until I was afraid that the food would get too cold. Then I knelt on the bed and kissed her on the forehead.

She looked up at me sleepily. "What happened?" she said.

"I brought you breakfast, Diana," I said.

Diana looked at me for a moment before her eyes cleared: then she started back suddenly. She looked around the room quickly and then sat up against the wall, holding the sheet against her chest.

"It's getting cold," I said. Diana turned to look at the tray of food and then shut her eyes as if the sight nauseated her.

"I'm going to wash my face," I said.

In the bathroom, for probably the first time in my life, I did not think about anything but what I was doing. As I washed my face, I washed my face, and I put on my socks as I put on my socks. Once a memory of throwing Abel down the stairs started to enter my mind, and guilt and terror rose up from my stomach to meet it, and the rape was trailing behind them, but I resolutely shut them all out.

When I went back into my room Diana was up and dressed. The food was untouched. I stood just inside the doorway, and Diana looked at me with a new depth of expression, and I imagined that I saw in her eyes love as well as pain. Nothing came out in her voice.

"I'm going to go home, Joseph," she said steadily.

"What do you want me to do, Diana?"

"Just walk me out, Joseph," she said. She was not looking at me.

I took her arm and we walked down the stairs. She did not

turn her head as we crossed the living room, and Abel, who was sitting on the couch, did not look up. I stood with her on the porch for a moment; then she left and I let her go.

I returned to the living room to announce that I would be back in ten minutes, and then I, too, left as quickly as I could. Unhappily, it seemed to me at the time, I found the doctor in his office and free.

"Good morning, Joseph," he said cheerfully. "How goes the war?"

When he said this I was suddenly no longer detached from myself: my mouth filled with spit and I could not meet his eyes.

"Can you come, please," I mumbled. He stood up immediately.

"What happened?" he demanded.

"Come," I said, still looking at the floor. The doctor moved abruptly and hustled me out the door. We walked toward my house.

"What happened?" he demanded again.

"He fell down the steps," I muttered. The doctor started to run but I grabbed his arm and held him back.

"Last night," I said. "He's all right."

The doctor slowed his pace somewhat and stared at me.

"He *fell*?"

My head was light and I was swallowing as rapidly as I could.

"I found him with Diana," I said.

The doctor looked at me sharply as I stared at the earth. We were approaching the door.

"Jesus," he said, "of her own free will?"

I stopped walking and bent over, hands on my knees.

"I don't think so," I said. I handed the doctor my key. He let himself in to examine the boy, and I threw up on the ground.

After I had recovered I went inside for a glass of water and then went into the cowshed. I think that the cow was able to smell the vomit on my breath. When I leaned over to scratch her nose and say hello, she lowed and pulled away from me.

"What's the matter with you, Cassandra?" I said plaintively. "Don't you know me?"

She lowed again, and it sounded to my ears as if she were saying "No."

When I went back inside with the milk I found the doctor waiting for me in the kitchen. He had put on the kettle to boil and was stirring loose tea in its canister with a spoon.

"I don't like this, Joseph," he said as I came in.

"Is he all right?"

Dr. Ericsson looked me in the eye now—we had been avoiding each other's faces since I walked into the room. His eyes were red, and it seemed as if he had started to cry.

"I don't like this, Joseph," he said again. "'Is he all right?' He's exactly the way he was when you found him, bruised and uncomfortable, not seriously injured, entirely silent. He didn't say a word to me."

It was very frightening to see Dr. Ericsson cry; it made my own eyes tear and I staggered with vertigo.

"What's the matter?" I said as I clutched the counter.

The doctor's eyes cleared and he took a step closer to me and spoke with deliberate force. "I don't like to see children thrown down stairs even if they ask for it," he said. "And I don't like to see you doing it. You are not competent to take care of this child, Joseph. This is not a fact that necessarily reflects on you—it may reflect more on the child. But who is to blame for the fact is the least important point."

I was leaning back where I stood and looking at the sink, the counter, the floor, and anything else that was far from the doctor's eyes.

He leaned in closer to me and spoke directly into my ear. "I want you to get the child out," he said.

Dr. Ericsson's command created in me a new current of guilt and apprehension, broad and terrible, that flowed through my mind almost constantly from then on; but it did not cause me to throw Abel out.

There were various secondary reasons for this. Among them was my fundamental inability to do things. I think that this came of a sort of ingrained, intellectually undeveloped fatalism. I say intellectually undeveloped because a belief in an inexorable fate, followed with logical consistency, should have no implications at all about whether to act or not act. Whatever you do will by definition be fated, and therefore thoughts of fate should have no bearing on what you do. But in my case it had always been my inclination—or at least always since I gave up being an artist—to do nothing and wait for things to happen.

Then, too, I told myself that I had a moral obligation to Abel, and to some extent I believed this. I believed that by taking the boy in and keeping him so long I had incurred an obligation to provide for him and take care of him. Naturally I also had an obligation not to throw him down the stairs, but once having done that I had an obligation to take care of him until he was better. I did believe this flimsy reasoning at the time, but as I say it is only a secondary reason.

The real reason I could not kick Abel out was because I was frightened. He was not only a part of my life, he had become a part of my mind, and I could not cut him out any more easily than I would cut off a hand or cut out feelings and memories. Furthermore, to the extent that he was responsible for the development of my own evil inclination—and I went on to do much worse than I have yet described—I believed and still believe that he had to be involved in my overcoming it. I could not send Abel to the orphanage and quietly revert to the way I was; my life with Abel would leave me changed, for good or ill, and I could not let him leave while that change in myself remained so much for the worse. I cannot deny the selfishness or cruelty of this reason—but that selfishness and that cruelty, too, were parts of that evil inclination I was trying to overcome.

But this is all really speculation, because at the time I did not think about it. I simply sat silently at my kitchen table drinking tea with the doctor. He did not speak to me except to say again, before he left, "I don't like it."

3

Sometime the next day I decided to bring my tools back to the basement. When I went into my study, where I had left them, I found my microscope out on my desk. The eyepiece was smudged and dirty, and there was a cracked slide thrown on the floor.

I felt very briefly annoyed, but this annoyance was soon overwhelmed by pity; I could still see Abel's hands trembling at the breakfast table, and I transferred this image to my desk and microscope. He was surely seeking an escape from his fear; I was older and physically stronger than he was, and would easily intimidate him once I demonstrated a willingness to attack him. But there was nothing to be done at the moment; I picked up my screwdriver and drill and walked downstairs.

I had taken only one step into the basement when I stopped in my tracks and smelled the air. The basement smelled thickly of urine. Again I was overwhelmed by pity: I pictured Abel, thrown into the basement and afraid to come out, finally being unable to control himself. I took a deep breath—as much to punish as to steady myself—and continued down the stairs.

But as I neared the bottom I slipped and fell, landing very painfully on my back on the steps. The basement did not smell because Abel had been afraid to leave it the other day: I had slipped on a puddle. The basement smelled because Abel had made a special trip to piss all over the stairs. Any pity or moderation I felt disappeared instantly before my anger. I shouted, "God damn it!"

I dropped my tools by the toolbox and ran up the basement stairs and then up to the second floor. My muscles were so tense that I had trouble changing my clothes.

"Fucking little bastard," I said. I went into my study to retrieve the lock and found Abel taking a book from the bookshelf. I restrained myself with difficulty from knocking him down.

"Put it down," I said. He replaced it on the shelf. He did not look afraid of me; he was nothing more than wary. This certainly did nothing to diminish my fury.

I grabbed him by his shoulder and pulled him out of the room. He jogged along next to me. I pushed him into his own room and took up a position in the doorway.

"This is your room," I said. Abel sat down calmly on the bed, and this made me still angrier. "This is your worry and your cage," I said. I waved the lock at him. "When I don't want to see you," I said, "I intend to lock you in. I am not going to clean this room and I don't care what you do to it. If you piss on the wall in here, the room will stink of it. It can sit there till it makes you sick."

Abel continued to look at me calmly, waiting patiently for me to finish. It was only with difficulty that I prevented myself from hitting him and moved out of the room; I slammed the door and put on the padlock. It was two o'clock in the afternoon. God save me: I left him locked in there till the following morning.

I did not have the stomach to do that very often. In the days that followed I put the lock on his door only at night, when he was asleep, and then only sometimes, when I remembered. In the course of my largely placid law career I had met a few criminals, and I had even visited prisons a few times—it had invariably made me sick.

I was no good at dispassionately assessing people; not, at least, when they were in the room. I was always grateful not to be a judge. Unless it was so patently insincere as to be offensive, a criminal's politeness and deference in the interview or the courtroom would always sway me. It did not matter if I knew him to be the perpetrator of disgusting murders: if he politely tipped his hat to me, I would flinch at the idea of locking him in a stone cell.

I know that this is a question of my own insecurity. For much of my life I was so convinced that I was not entitled to any respect or attention that I could not help liking anyone who gave me any. Sometimes this affection went against my better instincts; sometimes, indeed, I also disliked them. In fact it may be more accurate to say not that I could not help liking but that I could not help feeling *obliged to* anyone who treated me with attention or respect. Of course this makes no sense; even apart from the question of whether I personally was worth anything, it is unreasonable to consider that an unsolicited action can create obligation. But this was a lesson that I was very long in taking to heart.

I suppose that this raises the question of the origin of my insecurity. One easy answer is that I was, by my own count, a failure: I was no great painter. I may have given the impression that after my encounter with Mondrian I gave up the idea of painting entirely. I did give up the idea that I could be a success at it, the idea that it was possible for me to do it, the idea that there was any point in it. But, despite my belief at the time to the contrary, I never did quite get rid of the idea that it would have been the only worthwhile use of my life.

Even as a forty-year-old lawyer I imagined, in part of my mind, that anyone could see me for what I was, a failed painter. Even accepting the premise that my failure to paint had made my life a waste, I should have had no reasonable cause to feel ashamed about this before anyone but a successful painter, and

I never to my knowledge met one. But despite my own essential dishonesty—this is how I labeled my failure to disclose to everyone I met my spoiled ambition—I always took other people at their words, and if they presented themselves as confident, I believed that they had reasons for it. For that matter, how did I know that this or that person did not have a discreet atelier in the back of his house?

I know that all of this will sound ridiculous; it sounds ridiculous to me and I lived with it for decades. But what appears ridiculous when it is verbalized and viewed in the daylight of the conscious mind can be terrible and powerful when it remains in the gloomy subconscious. I think I can safely say that every human being's life is warped and restricted by a number of unconscious ideas that he would laugh at if he heard them described in so many words.

In general I allowed myself very little room for error. Perhaps this was the fault of my own native idealism; perhaps it was my parents' fault for making me anxious by taking it for granted that I would earn good grades in school. But whoever started me limping, it was my own fault that I spent decades sitting down. I could have learned to walk straight; instead I avoided it. I avoided commitment in any direction.

From the evening of my third day in the Museum of Modern Art until the morning when I found Abel at my door, I lived in a long gray night of indifference. I was neither intelligent nor stupid; I was neither interesting nor dull; and I was not, however many doors I held open or however patiently I waited, either evil or good.

CHAPTER NINE

1

This is how the month of December began.

"Now listen to me, you God-damned little maggot—I don't care if you touched my microscope or not. I only care that it's dirty. And as sure as there's a burning hell under my feet that I'll see you in someday, it doesn't matter to me what you say about it, either. From now on you had better appoint yourself the guardian of all things that are mine in this house, because the next time I find so much as a single speck of dust on the eyepiece of my microscope, I am going to beat you until you can't stand up.

"I will not stop to inquire into the rights and wrongs of the question, and I'm not going to wait for you to scream about it and plead your innocence, because I don't care. I'm making you responsible by definition. And I will grab you by the throat, throw you into the corner, and beat you until you can't stand up.

"Do you understand me?"

I gave the poor boy one final push into the wall, knocking his head, and he nodded and wiped his eyes. I locked him in his room. This drama took place in the late morning, and I left him locked in until dinnertime.

You can gather from this speech that the state of things in the green house had followed the weather. It was finally too cold to go out, and Abel and I were alone together for most of every day. I quickly lost my scruples and my self-consciousness and became a tyrant; Abel lost his bravado and began protesting his innocence of crimes that I caught him in the act of committing. (By "crimes" I mean those actions that, in this period, I took offense at.)

I hardly want to excuse myself, but only for the sake of clarity I want to emphasize that the viciousness was not only my fault. Abel would do something wrong, I would see it as a deliberate affront and lose my temper. He would be quiet for a day or two; then he would grow sullen; then he would do something wrong again. It was awful. Again for clarity I want to emphasize that the things he did wrong were most of them not similar to his dirtying my microscope, a peccadillo that could have been overlooked. They were most of them peccadilloes that could not be. He would leave dirty dishes on the kitchen floor. He would block open the back door with a brick and leave it so all night. He would knock the window shades off their brackets. For every one of these small mistakes he had a more or less plausible excuse, but the greater the number the less their plausibility.

I had finally gotten past his masks and I was seeing Abel's real feelings, but these feelings seemed to consist of nothing but anger, fear, and self-pity. I finally saw him cry, I heard him whine, I made him cower. It makes me unhappy now to write this because the writing calls up in my mind fragments of visual memory—Abel huddled in the corner, Abel wiping his free-flowing eyes—that, without context, are particularly unpleasant. I almost cannot bear to think of the padlock on his door.

But whenever I would have felt pity for the boy, the image of him with Diana came to my mind and prevented it. It is true that directly after that day in November I had felt remorse to the point of physical nausea for my reactions; but somehow I forgot about my role and remembered only Abel's, and this served as an insuperable wedge between us, blocking any human understanding. Below my conscious mind I think I felt terrible guilt for what I had done to the boy, but what I had done to him was in reaction to what he had done to me, so I even blamed him for my guilt.

In December, too, Abel for the first time told me about his past, although I think that he told me lies. In the quiet days between arguments and fights we would sometimes have nearly normal conversations at the kitchen table; not merely civil, they were sometimes engaging and almost friendly. They were probably the best conversations that two such careful and carefully dispassionate speakers could produce. But as the month went on he began to bring up, apropos of nothing, tales of former abuse.

One afternoon, for example, he said, "I lived with a priest once."

"Did you?"

I had quickly learned to recognize his sad stories, and I did not want to hear them. I could see no object in his telling them but to elicit sympathy, and since I could not produce this sympathy I felt only annoyance. I also found the way he told the stories curious and disturbing. When he first started, he told them casually, as if they were someone else's anecdotes that he had gotten secondhand; but the more of them he told, the more mechanical and disconnected he became as he told them. At the same time the stories themselves became always more explicitly self-pitying.

"He saved me," Abel said. In the case of this particular story Abel became perfectly detached as soon as he began it, and he did not hear the sarcastic tone of my replies.

"Do you mean that he baptized you?"

"He saved me from someone else," Abel said. "And he took me home with him. He lived in a small house. He taught me to read and was astonished at how quickly I learned."

"I'm sure he was."

"He wanted me to follow him into the priesthood," Abel said.

I laughed out loud at this but he did not hear.

"He taught me to read Latin," Abel said. He was not, as far as I could tell, really talking to me, and anyway I did not care. This conversation took place over breakfast, and when Abel got to Latin I stood up to wash my plate.

"But when I asked questions about doctrine he slapped me in the face," Abel said. I was running water on my plate to get off egg yolk.

"Father, Son, and Holy Ghost!" Abel shrieked suddenly, and he threw his plate into the kitchen cabinets, where it shattered.

You may imagine how I responded.

This shriek was the closest thing he ever gave to an indication of being moved by or indeed at all involved in his own stories. For the most part they seemed to amount to nothing more than a new attempt at attacking me; he had, after all, worn out his other methods. I say this only partly based on the way he told the stories; I have in mind also the fact that he stuck with his old methods when they continued to work.

Diana came over that afternoon. It was the first time I had seen her. When I let her in the front door Abel was sitting on a couch in the living room.

Her face was red from the cold, and strands of hair crossed it; she wore a brown suede jacket and a long purple scarf; she looked somewhat less beautiful but much more lovely than she usually did. Abel looked up from his book.

"I knew she'd come back," he said. Diana glanced over my shoulder at the boy.

I tried to block her from his sight with my body as I turned to speak to him. "Go to your room," I said. Abel stood up and approached the stairs.

"Would you like me to bring down the gavel first?" he said.

I was before him in an instant and I slapped him hard across the face. "Get upstairs," I said. I pushed him down into the stairs and stood ready to start kicking him if he did not ascend them quickly enough. He hurried up.

I returned to the living room and sat down; Diana sat down across from me.

For several moments we sat without speaking.

"I've been waiting for you, Joseph," she said at last.

"I'm sorry," I said. "I was waiting for you."

Diana nodded and looked down. Then she said, "What are we going to do?"

I thought about it.

"I don't know yet, Diana," I said. "Will you stay and have dinner?"

"What?"

"I love you, Diana," I said, "and I don't know what to do, but I think we should have dinner."

Diana looked at her fingernails. After several long seconds I went into the kitchen and began to take out pots and plates and food. Finally I leaned over the counter. "Will you stay, Diana?" I said.

Still looking at her fingernails, Diana nodded softly. After a moment she stood up and took off her coat.

When the food was ready and set out on the table, I put one serving on a tray and took it upstairs. I found Abel in his room using my Latin dictionary.

"What are you looking up?" I said.

"I'm just reading," he said. "Have you ever tried *posca,* Joseph?"

"Put it away and then come back here," I said.

Abel stood up leisurely and went out to follow my order as if it was not worth his time to argue about it.

When he came back in I put my hands on his shoulders and looked him in the eye. "Diana is staying for dinner," I said. "You will eat up here and remain in your room. I want to give you a warning in case you should ever see her again. I am only going to say this once. *If you mention the gavel, you will see the gavel.* Do you understand me?"

"Yes, sir," he said.

"Good."

I shut his door behind me and returned to join Diana at the table. She was looking down.

"I want to tell you—"

"Joseph—"

"—I want to tell you that I hold myself responsible, Diana, and that I will accept—"

"Joseph," she said, "I don't hold you responsible."

"Please—"

"Please," she said, looking at me for the first time, "Joseph, let's not talk about it, all right? Let's talk about something else?"

"Whatever you want," I said.

Diana said nothing. I cleared my throat.

"I wanted to tell you what I was thinking of last time I was in the forest," I said. Diana said nothing.

"I was thinking of the first walk we took together, and how we imagined the trees, and I started thinking of new ones." I cleared my throat again; I had never felt more self-conscious in my life. "I imagined the trees as a nomadic tribe of old sages that walks so slowly that we can't see it," I said.

Diana looked down at her plate and played with her fork.

"They would grow up and live and die while traveling," she said softly, "and the tribe would have more identity than any single tree."

"Yes," I said, "and they would whisper among themselves of

their arboreal Jerusalem, though none of them had seen it for tens of thousands of years."

The corners of her mouth turned up.

"I like that," she said. "They wouldn't even remember which direction it lay in."

"Beautiful," I said. "Your turn."

"I imagine the trees," she said, "as the long green arms of the earth, on which she grows many fingers, and on the fingers many nails, and on the nails many needles, all trying to recover the sky that will not embrace her."

"Beautiful," I said again. "And in the morning, at dawn, the sky rests closer to the earth than at any other time, and she remembers the early morning once long ago when they embraced, and she remembers when she gave birth to the animals, to the fish, and to men, and the tall treetops quiver with desire as they are caressed by the early clouds, but they never touch his face."

"Because the sky is jealous," Diana said, "the sky is jealous because the earth will not share their children; she holds them close to her breast even after they die."

I thought about this.

"He doesn't realize," I said, "that they're with him all the time."

From these trees we moved easily into a normal conversation. I left our dishes in the sink, and together we left the house; we had decided to take a walk into the forest, but we realized as soon as we were out that it was too cold, and so I simply walked Diana home. But this time when she said that she did not want me to go back, I did not.

2

The following morning the sun streamed in the windows and I was happy. I felt that there was nothing better in the world than the warm sleeping body of a woman against you under the covers and the air cold out above them. Diana's face did not become red or pressed with sleep this time: instead her skin became clearer, her brown freckles more subtle, her features more sculpted and classical. She seemed in the early morning to have a Roman nose.

I kissed her eyelids, not meaning to wake her, but the eyelids fluttered open. She stared at me with an expression still better than a smile, and when I tried to kiss her again, she clenched her eyes shut and pressed her face into my chest. She caught my right leg in her own two and whispered in my ear. "It's too early!" she said.

I touched her naked white back beneath the cover. "It's full daylight," I whispered back.

"I don't care," she said, "we're not getting up."

"Never?"

"Never," she said. "We'll spend the rest of our lives here. At least the rest of the day."

"What will we do in bed all day?"

Diana laughed at me, the answer to this question being so obvious, and it was midmorning before we went downstairs. Together we sat at her kitchen table eating toast and drinking tea, quietly laughing at each other. When I stood up to put the dishes away, Diana stood up, too; she poked me in the side and blew in my ear to annoy me. "You're going to go home, aren't you, Joseph?" she said.

"I probably should."

"Have you got some other girls waiting for you?"

"Oh," I said, "not more than six or seven."

Diana walked me out holding hands and we kissed on the porch before I left.

I came into the green house to find Abel sitting at the table with his book. He knew that I was only just coming in; he looked up at my approach and smiled. "I'm glad she's finally treating you right, Joseph," he said. "I could have told you two months ago that all she wanted was a spanking."

I cannot remember if it was a punch or a flat blow with the knuckles that I gave to the back of his head, but I do remember that he laughed. I gave him another and another until he stopped laughing; I left him with his head in his hands.

There was a knock at the back door then, and I opened it to find the doctor. I had just beaten a child into a state of semiconsciousness, and I should have been afraid to answer the door. But my behavior with Abel had at this point a life of its own, and neither his remark nor my response to it had even affected the glowing mood that being with Diana had left me in.

"Good morning, Michael," I said, "what a pleasure to see you."

Dr. Ericsson looked past me at the boy with his head uneasily in his hands.

"What's wrong with him?" he said. I smiled.

"Don't you say 'good morning'?"

The doctor hardened his eyes.

"What is wrong with the boy, Joseph?" he said.

"He didn't sleep well. Would you like to come in?"

"Yes," he said shortly. I stepped out of his way, and he walked directly to Abel. "Pick up your head, Abel," he said softly.

Abel looked at him with bleary eyes. "Go fuck yourself, Sambo," he muttered.

I was appalled—remember that I did not, at the time, know anything about what had gone on between them two when I was not there. This was the first such term that I had heard out of the boy's mouth. But the doctor doubled my admiration for him by being entirely deaf to it.

He held Abel's face gently in his hands and opened his eyelids to look into his eyes. "Stand up, boy," he said, but he helped Abel to his feet. He produced a small light from his pocket and, holding Abel's chin in his left hand, he shined the light carefully in his eyes.

"What's your name?" the doctor asked him.

"Julius Caesar," Abel said.

"Don't play around with me right now," the doctor said. "What's your name?"

"Abel Rufous."

"What's my name?"

"Ericsson."

"Move your arms and legs," the doctor said, and Abel shrugged his shoulders and took a step in place. All this time the doctor had been holding on to Abel's shoulders; now he let him go, and Abel remained where he had been set, swaying slowly. The doctor put one arm around him to lead him to the living room and set him on the couch.

"Just sit here and take it easy for a little while," the doctor told him. Leaving Abel he returned to me, grabbed my shirt, and pulled me into the kitchen. "Did insomnia give the boy his concussion?" he demanded.

"You're the doctor," I said.

The doctor's look of disgust at this answer filled me with shame—not over what I had done to Abel as such but only over provoking the doctor's disgust—but I did not feel that I could move from my position.

"He said something about Diana," I said. Once this was said I felt still more compelled to explain. "He wouldn't stop laughing," I added. "I couldn't—"

"Shut up," the doctor said. "Sit down."

I sat.

"Joseph," he said, "what did I tell you the last time I was here?"

I could not speak.

"I told you to get the child out. I told you that you were not competent to care for this child. I also said that it did not reflect on you, but it does. You have lived alone all your life and are frankly too immature to take care of a child. You beat him up because he made an obnoxious remark? Jesus Christ, Joseph, do you have any idea of the things the boy has said to me when I've examined him?"

Of course I did not.

"Why didn't you say anything?"

The doctor looked at me for a long moment before he spoke. "'Come see the diagnosing nigger,'" he said.

"My God, Michael," I said, "I'm so—"

"I think my favorite was 'goddamn dancing bush nigger faggot.' 'Shit-eating jungle bunny' really isn't very creative."

I could almost feel the blood draining from my face. "My God, Michael," I said, "I'm so sorry; I had no idea that he—"

"Don't change the God-damned subject!" the doctor shouted. "I am making a point. These are some of the many terrible things this child has said to me. But do you see me beating him in the head?"

I looked down in shame, but after a second I became aware that the doctor had not meant his question only rhetorically. "No," I whispered.

"No," he said, "you don't. Why not? Because, Joseph, the boy does not say these things only because he is a hateful little demon filled with bile. He is that, and that is part of the reason, but it is the smaller part. He says these things to provoke you into a reaction, to manipulate and control you. The fact that the boy feels compelled to provoke anger in other people in this singularly unpleasant way is without question his flaw, whether native or beaten in, but he is a child and he may grow out of it. He is in any case smaller than I am, and he is smaller than you are. But the fact that you participate in it, the fact that you allow yourself to be provoked and manipulated by a dirty-mouthed teenager is your flaw, and you do not seem to be growing out of it. Are you following me, Joseph?"

"Yes," I whispered.

"All along you have been treating this boy as a friend of your own age, and this is what it has come to. I know that in law school you must have come across the concept of disinterest. But evidently you either did not come to understand it or did not think that it applied here. Disinterest is never more important than in the treatment of children. They are weaker than you and more malleable. Do you understand, Joseph?"

"Yes."

"I don't like sending a child to an orphanage any more than you do; I would prefer any other possible solution. But there is none. He cannot stay in your house and he cannot stay in this town. You should have called the police when you first found him but you did not, and it's too late now. There's nothing else to do."

The doctor had begun to speak to himself as if I were not in the room, and this annoyed me just enough to wake me up to my own arguments. "You're absolutely right, doctor," I said.

Dr. Ericsson returned from pacing with his own thoughts and sat down.

"But you also don't know everything. I told you that I found him with Diana, but I didn't tell you how."

The doctor sighed impatiently and looked away.

"Listen to me, Michael," I said, and he looked up and met my eyes. "I found her in Abel's room, naked on his bed, lying on her stomach and crying as he raped her with the handle of my gavel." I spoke this sentence bitterly, but it was bitter only with my momentary anger; I did not while speaking it really think about what it meant.

The doctor, however, turned slightly pale and sank into a chair.

"I do not want to be rude, doctor, forgive me, but what would you do if it had been your wife?"

The doctor was shocked—I had made my point.

"I would probably murder him, Joseph," he said. "I know at least that I would want to."

"There you are."

"But I wouldn't keep him in my house, Joseph—Jesus! It's not your place to be a jailer to him!"

"Why not? Someone has to be Cain."

"Cain did not have recourse to the machinery of the state."

"Damn it," I said. I stood up to kick the wall. "That isn't the point. It's completely irrelevant. I took the boy in and I assumed a responsibility. Nothing that he does or that I do—"

"I'm afraid that it's because you've come to like having someone to beat."

"I don't *like* it," I said. "But if, for example, Diana comes over for dinner, and Abel offers again to go and fetch the gavel, then I probably will hit him again. And until he runs away or *I* decide otherwise, he will continue to live in this house."

Dr. Ericsson stood up and seemed to spend several moments considering what he could say. Finally he looked at his watch. "I'm going to look at him again," he said. "I want you to check him every two hours for the next two days. Get me immediately if you have trouble waking him."

After he had checked on Abel in the living room, Dr. Ericsson let himself out the front door.

3

The three weeks that followed this conversation were the most painful weeks that I have had to pass in my life. But I will find it difficult to portray this fact with any reality because nothing at all happened. I woke up in the morning and brushed my teeth and bathed; I used the toilet; I got dressed; I walked downstairs and made breakfast. I ate with Abel. I went back up to my study and opened a book or took out a piece of paper to write a letter. I walked downstairs and made lunch; I went back up to my study. It continued this way for three weeks. But physical facts are of themselves nearly meaningless. I could say that they approach hyperbolically the absolute absence of significance. It is our perception of them that gives them meaning: it is not in life as such but in our feelings about it that we live. And in those three weeks I felt as I imagine a man walking up the gallows steps must feel.

For the first few days things were especially quiet. Abel recovered only slowly from his concussion. He slept all night in bed and through most of the day on the living room couch. I kept him covered with a blanket, I brought him his meals, and I helped him down the stairs in the morning and up the stairs in the evening. I checked him every two hours. I believed that he was inventing his incapacity; I did not think that there was so much middle ground between what can be cured by a night's sleep and what cannot be cured. But I was in no position to accuse him, and I would not have wanted to. I was glad that I did not have to talk to him.

He felt better after a few days and began walking up and down by himself, sitting up on the couch, reading books and writing in penny notebooks that he had bought himself at the store. (Later I saw that he had filled those notebooks with meaningless scratches.) He was perfectly civil to me and I was perfectly civil to him. I do not know what it was that made me so tensely afraid or how I knew, if I did, what was coming. I think that with the last beating I had given him I had simply stretched myself as far as I could stretch and committed myself to a final course. I think also that I could see the slightly increased readiness with which Abel held his frame as he read, and I knew that it would lead to nothing good.

It is particularly hard for me to resolve my general impression of those three weeks after the beating with my memory of Diana from the same time. I was like a seventeen-year-old in love. It is true that I did not think about her in every last available moment, and I did not even see her every day; but when I did see her I was giddy. I could not be near her without touching her, she could not speak without delighting me. I was like two men. When Diana was there, I was entirely happy and forgetful of all else.

Three weeks from the day I had last beaten Abel I went to visit Diana at her house. It was warmer outside than it had been for a month and I wanted to spend the afternoon in town. After I had washed the lunch dishes I went and found Abel on the couch.

"I'm going to go into town for the afternoon," I said. "I'll be home in time to make dinner."

Abel nodded silently without looking up from his book. It will seem unbelievable, I suppose, if I say that he was reading the Bible, but I am fairly certain of my recollection. In any case it does not matter very much; he did not look up and I went out.

I walked into town with the intention of going directly to Diana's, but when I saw the doctor's door I decided to stop in and say hello. I wanted to make certain that, despite our recent argument, we remained friends. My bad three weeks in the green house with Abel Rufous were not improved any by the way I had parted with my friend Michael Ericsson.

I found the doctor's office closed and a note on the door saying that he had gone to visit a patient in Penley. If I had not seen his door in the first place, I would not have thought of stopping, but once having seen it and decided to call on him, finding him gone made me feel very unsettled. I felt as if we had just had our argument and settled nothing. But there was nothing to be done, so I continued on to Diana's. Diana was in; she opened the door; the doctor retreated to the back of my mind.

Once as a young man I wanted to describe to a friend how I felt about a certain girl. It was not a girl that I had ever declared myself to, but I certainly thought about her a lot. I asked my friend to imagine a large party attended by everyone in the world that he knew. I told him that at such a party there would be many people he would avoid: spending time with these would mean nothing more to him than missing the company of others. Then there would be the close friends whose company he would enjoy and value but who would not make him forget entirely the other close friends in the room. I said that if I were at such a party with this girl, I could leave the hall with her and happily spend the whole day sitting in the stairwell without once missing anyone.

This is how I felt when Diana opened her door and smiled at me. It is true that I remembered my unsettled argument with the doctor and the tension with Abel, but for the moment they did not seem to matter. I had again caught Diana baking. She had on a white apron and held a wooden spoon, and I kissed her high on the back of her cheekbone.

"Come in, Joseph," she said. "I'm making you a cake."

"I already owe you one cake," I said.

"It doesn't matter," she said. "After I give it to you, you can give it to me, and then we'll be even."

I laughed.

"I guess mathematics is not your strong point," I said.

"Sit down and be quiet," she ordered me. "It's almost ready."

I sat down on the couch and watched Diana return to the kitchen.

"Do you want to have dinner here tonight, Joe?" she called out. It gave me a thrill—a literal thrill down my back, through my legs to my toes—to hear her call me Joe.

"I want to," I said. I felt a quick sting. "But I should go back to make dinner for . . . I ought to go back."

There was silence from the kitchen, and I felt suddenly miserable.

"Diana," I cried out, "just let me run back before we eat, I'll only be gone ten minutes."

After I had said this Diana came sailing out of the kitchen toward me. "I'm sorry," she said, "I was in the oven. What did you say?"

I reached out to put my arm around her leg, my hand on her lower back. My anxiety disappeared. "I said that I ought to go back for dinner."

Diana leaned down and kissed me on the top of the head. "That's all right, Joe," she said. "I'll just sit in my room and cry."

She laughed at me then because for a moment I believed her.

"I love you, Diana," I said.

"I love you, Joe."

She stood over me for a moment with her fingers in my hair, and then she sat down in my lap.

I do not remember what we spoke about, and I do not suppose that any of it would mean anything on paper. I remember only that we sat happily as we were until we smelled something burning and Diana leaped up and ran into the kitchen.

"Diana," I called out, "do you hear that?"

"What is it?"

"It sounds like the town bell is ringing," I said. It began to grow louder, and I was correct: it was the frantic ringing of the high town bell. I stood up uneasily and walked into the kitchen.

"When do they ring that bell, Diana?" I asked.

Diana looked up at me from the ash-black cake in her hands with a face so forlorn that I was almost frightened. I took her in my arms.

"I ruined the cake, Joseph," she said.

"I ruined it," I said. "I interrupted you. It's my fault."

She pressed her face into my shoulder.

Meanwhile the bell continued to toll, and as Diana broke our embrace and wiped her eyes there was a quick burst of knocking against the front door. I strode quickly out to open it.

There was no one on the porch when I opened the door, but there were people milling in the street and a few running, and I saw the shopkeeper's son two houses down: he was knocking on each door and running to the next. Diana's house was not far from the edge of Bettley, but everyone was walking past her house toward the woods—toward my own house.

"What's going on?" I shouted. I could barely hear myself.

One of my townsmen drifting slowly past raised his arm and pointed at the sky: there was black smoke rising from among the trees where the green house stood.

In a single instant my heart fell through my belly as I imagined two things: I imagined Abel as an arsonist, and I imagined him burned to death, and I did not know which I preferred. Then, of course, I imagined myself homeless in January.

"Diana," I screamed, "stay here," and I leaped off the porch and began running. The townsmen in the street all got out of my way and it took me only a moment to slip around the bend in the road and come upon my house. It was not burning.

I stood with my hands on my knees trying to catch my breath. The house was not burning. I decided that there must be a tree on fire in the forest, and they were afraid of its spreading; but there had been no storm, so the only way a tree could be burning was if someone had lit it.

But when I caught my breath and stood up, and then I turned my head, I saw that my cowshed had burned almost to the ground, and it was being left to finish burning. My neighbors were carefully scorching the grass around it and wetting the nearest trees.

Diana appeared beside me and caught my left hand in her hand. "What happened?" she asked. She had come directly to me and had not looked at anything else. I pointed silently to the burnt shed and we watched the remnants burn down.

"Where is Cassandra?" she asked. I let go of her hand and approached the fire. The shopkeeper was standing back a little further than the other men, supervising or pretending to supervise.

"Where is the cow?" I asked him. He shook his head.

"This was a cowshed," I said. "I keep a cow. Where is she?"

"She was inside," he said.

The shed was almost burned down to nothing now; it was only a black pile of smoldering ashes. I stood back to wait.

"Where is Abel?" Diana said.

"Fuck him."

"Joseph," she said, "I'll stand and watch here."

Diana's expression was guileless and inflexible. I kissed her and went into the house.

"Abel!" I shouted. "Where are you?"

When he did not answer I stomped up the stairs.

"Abel! Where are you?"

He did not answer. I continued to yell his name as I looked in my bedroom, in my study, and in his bedroom. I did not look in closets or under beds because it did not occur to me that he would be hiding: if he wanted to hide from me he could go out into the forest. But then, too, he might go into the basement.

I ran down the steps to the ground floor and paused only for a moment to catch my breath.

"Abel!" I shouted again. The door to the basement opened.

"Here I am, Joseph," he said.

I did not like the way he was moving. As I spoke I clenched my teeth together to keep myself from shouting. "Are you all right, Abel?" I asked. "Why are you wearing your coat?"

"The serpent beguiled me," he said, "and I did eat."

The muscles of my left arm tightened painfully and my fingers bent into a fist. Abel turned and began walking slowly up toward his room and I left him.

Across the road only two or three men remained, kicking at the ashes of my cowshed. The fire was out. I approached them glaring.

"Thank you," I said coldly.

"Just want to make sure it doesn't flare up again," one answered.

"There's nothing left to burn," I said. "Thank you."

They shrugged off my ingratitude and left. Diana came beside me again and put her arm around my shoulder. I hardly noticed: I was staring at a shape beneath the remnants of the roof.

"Did you find him?" she said.

I moved forward and began kicking away burnt fragments of wooden beams.

"Did you find him, Joe?"

I could see the body of Cassandra, my cow, fallen on its side in the debris, but it did not look right.

"Joseph," Diana said.

I kicked at the fragments, and the ashen wood turned to powder that floated up to mark my clothing and choke me.

"Diana," I said, "there's a shovel in my basement."

She took one step and then hesitated.

"What's the matter, Joseph?"

"Please, Diana," I said. I looked at her urgently, and she ran off for the shovel. I could see the outline of Cassandra's body but it was not complete.

When Diana came running back I took the shovel from her hands and began to move the ashes carefully from the great corpse. Diana stood by my shoulder.

The cow's skin was scorched and in places bubbled, and for

a moment I shuddered to think of any creature burning to death—but of course she had not.

Diana gasped.

I uncovered the decapitated body of my murdered animal in the ashes of her shed on blood-soaked ground. When the body was clear I fell to my knees in the black ash and wiped small pieces of soot from her neck. Pieces of burnt skin clung to my fingers.

I could see clearly despite the effects of the fire that it was no clean cut: though shriveled and blackened, the ragged pieces of flesh that hung from her body were unmistakable. The neck bone had clearly been hacked to pieces. I looked around the ground blindly, hoping to come on some excuse or explanation. Diana had turned away; she was leaning on her knees gagging. A small glinting light caught my eye, and I uncovered the blade of my saw left on the ground.

I stood up covered in ashes. Somehow I saw a small streak of red on the trunk of a nearby tree: I stepped into the forest and stared into the glassy eyes of the cow's head that had been thrown there. I was covered in black ashes.

"Diana," I said. I should say that I croaked—no voice came. She faced me with tears in the corners of her eyes, and I took her shoulders in my hands, ruining her light gray coat.

"Thank you," I said, "lovely Diana. Please go home. Go home. I will see you tomorrow. Please."

I left her standing there and crossed the road. I wiped off the worst of the ashes at the door and then went in to wash my hands. I walked down the basement stairs. There was an old leather suitcase of my father's effects that the railroad had tied a rope around. I held the metal shovel in my hands.

CHAPTER TEN

1

As we walked I noticed Abel pulling at the cuffs of his shirt as if to cover his hands with his sleeves. I did not know if it was a nervous gesture or only a reaction to the cold. I asked him what was the matter with him.

He did not answer me immediately, and for several minutes we walked silently on the half-frozen ground.

"I was raised," he said at last, "in an emotionally cold household by parents who were more interested in their own problems and in each other than in me. I didn't have any brothers or sisters, and I wouldn't let myself have any close friends because I didn't credit anyone with the ability to understand me. I was exceptionally intelligent, but that intelligence interfered with my ability to feel and express my own emotions. I developed an excessive capacity for self-absorption and self-pity, and whatever native ability I had to empathize with and feel for other human beings withered away from disuse. You might say that my life so far has been defined by the attempt to simultaneously win my parents' affection and prove to them that I don't need it. I wanted to be world famous, so that they could not ignore me, but gain that fame in some way that had nothing to do with them and everything to do with my own natural merit. To that end, when I was thirteen years old, Joseph, I decided to become a painter.

"Because I was interested not in painting as such but merely in its consequences, it never occurred to me to really look at the world around me, let alone pick up a pencil and sketch something, let alone actually learn how to paint. Instead I developed what I would have thought of as an adult identity based on my presumed superiority to the rest of humanity as a painter and an artist. But then one day, one fateful day, one terrible, awful day, I strayed into a museum. Whatever was I thinking. And in that museum, Joseph, I saw evidence of actual painting, the product of real interest and real talent, and it destroyed what I had trained myself to consider my life's ambition, because I saw that it was entirely out of my reach. I was forced to admit to myself that I was no kind of painter, and therefore that I had no kind of superiority to anyone else, that I was a fraud, that I was without use or originality, and so I gave up all my ambition, not merely to be a painter but to be anything at all, and I sank myself into the weak, indifferent middle of humanity.

"Then I spent several decades drifting along pointlessly, thinking nothing, saying nothing, and doing nothing, until I was practically a walking pile of dust. But however miserable I was, I was far too afraid to do anything about it, and I convinced myself that it was because I had a sort of religious fatalism, instead of facing the truth, that I was just small and weak and frightened. What's the matter with me, Joseph, is that I gave up being alive twenty-five years ago, and by now I've gotten to the point where I'd rather snivel and cry because it's cold out than put on a fucking sweater or go inside. That's what's fucking the matter with me."

I, for my part, did not answer this immediately, and again we walked silently for several minutes.

"I wanted to know," I said at last, "why you're pulling your sleeves down like that."

Abel answered without pause. "Because I'm cold," he said, "you fucking genius."

"Why—"

"My body is cold, my breath is cold, my blood is cold, my heart is cold, my bones are cold, my eyes are cold. Why don't you ever stop talking? There isn't a philosophy of being cold and talking about it doesn't make me warm. Bearing in mind that I'm cold is not going to let me dance across the forest without a fucking coat. I'm cold because I'm cold, you fucking pansy, it doesn't mean anything."

Abel coughed roughly and spat. We stopped walking for a moment, and I stuck the point of my shovel into the ground. We were already three or four miles north of Bettley; the pines here were fiercer and more distant. I took off my jacket and draped it around the boy's shoulders. He accepted it without a word and we continued walking.

I jumped up and down in the freezing air to try to speed up

my heart and only then noticed for the first time that it was already beating loud and fast. I slung the rope, which I had tied to the shovel's handle, across my shoulders and galloped across the pine needles to catch up with Abel.

"Where wast thou, Josephina," he said.

"What?"

We were walking together now but we were both staring straight ahead.

"Where wast thou," he said, "when I laid the foundations of the earth. Canst thou draw out leviathan with an hook."

I did not say anything, and we walked in silence. After several freezing minutes Abel answered himself. "The answers," he burst out, "are as follows, one, where wast thou, you were nowhere, and two, canst thou, no, you can't."

I stopped walking and plunged my shovel into the dirt.

"How far are we from Bettley?" he said.

"Far enough."

I do not want to sound as if I am trying to justify myself with physical signs of a superego, so I will say once that my hands were trembling and my stomach turned over and leave it at that.

"How far away is New Salem?"

"We're closer to there than we are to here," I said.

Abel took off the coat I had given him and held it out to me and I took it. He turned away to look at a tree. It was an elm tree, the only deciduous tree I had ever seen in the pine forest. As Abel stood quietly resting his eyes on the black elm bark I stood behind him. I had let the coat fall to the ground. I tried, as I untied the rope from the shovel handle, to imagine myself looping it twice around Abel's neck and pulling the ends as he

strangled and struggled. It was a thick, coarse rope, and all I succeeded in doing at first was picturing how the fibers would
scrape my palms. But once having thought of this I could not
fail to realize how the rope would affect the boy's neck, and this
led to imagining the struggle.

"It's interesting," Abel said, "how the bark of an elm looks
cracked and broken but is actually a perfect seal over the heart of
the tree."

Having dropped the rope I now stood holding only the short
steel shovel. I imagined whacking Abel on the back of the head.
I thought I could do that once. But once would not do, I would
have to do it again, in the end I would have to break and bloody.
I swallowed the spit that filled my mouth, put down the shovel,
and approached the boy. It struck me that the shovel and the
rope were both equally cowardly: he was mine and I would
have to touch him.

As Abel started to turn I threw one arm across his throat and
pulled him toward me. For a moment, as if he did not believe
me, he did not resist, but then he began to thrash fiercely and
bared his teeth. We fell to the ground and moved together. I do
not know how long the struggle went on and I cannot say who
did what—I lost all sense of time and identity. There was nothing but the fight, not even any distinction between the fighters.
We were a single animal, forgetful of the world, struggling with
itself in a terrible fit. But all through this, one wrist pressed into
one throat, and finally it ended and our bodies fell apart: mine
still trembling, Abel's dead.

When I had caught my breath I sat up and knelt beside him.
I think that I imagined he was at rest; I felt nothing. Abel's skin

had lost some of its color in our past few weeks indoors, and I was just able to make out some red scratches under his chin. They would not be noticeable to anyone not looking for them. I held my steel watch under his nose, and it was as I stared at its unfogged cover that terror and panic finally came on me.

They surged up through my flesh, and a rushing started in my ears that grew constantly louder. But at this moment, for the only time in my life, I could have thanked God for making me a lawyer.

"Be still," I said sharply. "Now is not the time for it. If you want to feel terror or have second thoughts, you have to do it before the victim is dead. There's no point now. You can't help him. You can't do anything for him but bury him cleanly. The only thing left is to be calm and rational and take care of yourself."

The terror crested again but I slapped it down.

"You are not my conscience," I said, "you are only animal fear," and whatever it was, conscience or fear, it was gone.

It took me several hours to dig a grave. I made it as deep as I practically could. I had no fear of anyone finding the body in the massive forest, even if someone had reason to look for it, but I felt averse on principle to half measures, and anyway it seemed more respectful. It was the least I could do.

As I straightened out Abel's clothes preparatory to lowering him down, I found his gold pen with the initials LMS. I turned it over and looked at it as if seeing it for the first time. All this time, after my first brief moment of fear, I had been calm, methodical, and remorseless. I had thought about literature while I dug up the hard earth. But as I looked at that gold pen, a thought occurred to me that broke the camel's back. It is really a lovely pen, I thought, and there is hardly any sense in wasting it.

I staggered five or six steps from the body before I threw up. I managed to walk back and slip the pen in Abel's pocket as I started crying; then I spent twenty or thirty minutes that must have been as bad as any hell. But I am glad that I spent them, because I think that I expressed and thereby conquered every pain and regret in me, not only from Abel's stay but from my whole adult life and perhaps even from childhood. It is lucky for me that sound does not carry far in the pine forest.

When I had finished crying, I lowered Abel into the hole with my jacket and then lay on the ground and reached in to straighten his legs. I found as I pulled the jacket back out that he had slipped two crumpled pieces of paper into one of the pockets. They were pages torn out of my Bible; on them were the verses in Job that he had quoted to me. I got on the ground again to lay the papers on his breast and cross his arms over them.

In his grave in the falling night Abel looked just as he had the morning that I had found him on my porch, and standing looking at him I felt something of what I had felt for him then. For a long time I stood there not wanting to leave. Finally it got too cold.

"God rest you," I said, and then I covered him with dirt and turned back.

2

I told Abel at one point that I did not know why tuberculosis interested me so much, and I believe that I have said the same thing earlier in this book. It is true that I do not know *why* it fascinated me, but it is disingenuous of me to say so, because I can easily say *what* fascinated me.

I was fascinated by the age of the disease. Tuberculosis has coexisted with man for as long as he has recorded history, and indeed, it would be impossible to say which is older. It has been part of the human condition for as long as there has been a human condition.

I was fascinated by the contradictions of the disease. Tuberculosis is not a particularly virulent infection: a reasonable amount of ventilation in the home, a few open windows, will keep it away. But it lurks in dirty dark corners, and when people live close together it spreads like fire. Those that it infects may die quickly and suddenly; they may die after protracted suffering; they may be sentenced by the doctors to death and then go on, as my great-grandfather did, to live another seventy years. They may be sent north, to Bettley, for example, to breathe the clean air as they take their pills, and find after a few years that the disease has entirely passed. Or they may spend years without a symptom and then be stricken terribly. Many people live full lives without experiencing the disease even indirectly; but at any given time a quarter of the earth's population is infected with it. Millions die of it every year, but it has never created the sort of social upheaval or apocalyptic terror that is commonly caused by other plagues, because it is quiet, discreet, and accepted. It has always been a part of the human condition and so it is taken for granted. Some doctors dream of eliminating it, but it is difficult to imagine life without it.

It can deform and disfigure, but it can also beautify: there is the consumptive beauty as well as the scrofulous terror. The ethereal pallor ascribed to dancers and fairies is the beauty of a terrible disease. It has been considered romantic and appalling, often both at once. It would be impossible to count the great poets and artists who were shaped by the disease, by its symptoms and the necessities of treating those symptoms, by the enforced awareness of mortality, and almost certainly, I think, in deeper and more subtle ways. Uncountable are the poetic geniuses it has caused to flower and then gone on to extinguish.

I was fascinated by its evolution—drugs are developed to combat it, and it learns how to combat the drugs. I wondered whether each new treatment regimen is merely a change or is an advance, whether, that is, the disease is making us wiser and stronger by forcing us to fight it. I was fascinated by its vectors. It is fundamentally a disease of social relations; it is transmitted in spit and phlegm, and it is nearly impossible for a single human living alone to catch it. For it to pass from one person to another, they must live in close contact for months. For it to pass among a hundred or a thousand people, all that is necessary is close quarters. The closer and warmer the ranks of humanity, the worse the spread of disease, as if a greater good must logically be matched by a greater evil.

I was fascinated by the very nature of infectious disease. The bacteria invade the body, they affect it, they change it, they turn it to their own purposes—they become part of it. At some point they must cease to be invaders and become citizens, if not fully public-spirited ones, of the bodily republic. For what essential difference is there between them and any other bacterium or cell? Only that the others have been there longer. This raises the question of whether there is any stability or solid foundation to human ego and identity, whether there is an unchanging core that can be called individual, and the answer appears to be no. And what control, then, do we have over our actions? None. The human mind is a brilliant creation, and it can convince itself that it has reasons for doing anything, even for coughing, but the fact remains that a consumptive does not cough because *he* wants to but because the mycobacteria want him to. The proof of this is that he may take the opposite course, he may convince himself that it is absolutely necessary that he not cough, he may become entirely aware of the disease that he carries, he may deplore it, he may know that coughing will not help him but will only make him worse, he may resolve never to cough again—but he will cough anyway. Disease is not something you do but something that happens to you; and the only difference that I can see between disease and sin is that one of them manifests more subtly than the other.

When I began reading about tuberculosis, the first thing to catch my eye and fascinate me was the name "the king's evil." In England until the eighteenth century it was believed that scrofula—a term once interchangeable with tuberculosis that has come to mean more specifically tuberculosis of the glands—could be cured by the touch of the sovereign. I did not spend much time thinking about this belief literally because it is absurd on its face— What about pretenders to the throne? What about kings who are lieges of emperors? Does the cure depend on the physical transmission of some royal quality, and if so, could it be removed and bottled, and if not, why could the king not decide by an act of will to cure all scrofula everywhere? As a metaphor, however, the sovereign's touch seemed to me to be a moving and powerful idea. Most obviously, for example, it stands for a Christian idea of divine grace and forgiveness. It argues that the body is determined by the soul. For a long time my favorite way to think of the king's evil was as the salutary influence a good adult could have on a misdirected child, but I have learned better than that.

I finally came to think of the king's evil in an entirely different way. I look at it now as evil committed, or at least allowed, by the king. A king that rules his country by divine right must also be responsible for whatever goes on in it, even natural disease. It is the nature of his position. Try as he may to do only good, somewhere in his domain someone will die of a hideous disease, and that is his evil. Someone will be murdered and that is his evil. And contrarily if he is vicious and cruel and tries to do only wrong, still, somewhere in his domain there will grow flowers, and men and women will fall in love. These are his goods. And the goods, I think, could not be good without the evil, nor the evil without the good, for they shadow each other: they are indispensable to each other.

3

By the time I had gotten home, washed the shovel, tied the rope back around its suitcase, washed myself, and changed my clothes, it was nearly dawn. I decided that it was more sensible to go without sleep entirely, so I made myself a pot of coffee and sat down in the kitchen to read a pile of newspapers from the past few weeks that I had not gotten to yet.

It is a wonderful property of the dawn that it washes away everything that has happened in the night. I would not have denied that I had, in that night, created a cavern in my soul that would remain there forever; but sitting in my kitchen under the bright morning with a cup of coffee and a newspaper I was just as confident that I could happily forget about the cavern for the rest of my life.

The only thing I felt was a little at loose ends—for the first time in months my day was my own and free, and I had forgotten what to do with it. I decided to have a dinner party.

This inspiration made me so excited—so manic, I should probably say—that I ran right up to my study to write out invitation cards for Michael and Diana. No sooner had I sat down and taken out the paper than I jumped up again to go invite them in person. I hastily put on a nice dark suit and ran out of the house. I forgot to wear a coat, but I was running quickly and I did not feel the cold.

"Michael, Michael," I said, "where are you?"

I was banging on the door of his office, but it did not seem open yet. I continued banging until he came up behind me.

"Good morning, Joseph," he said. "Why are you dressed up?"

"For dinner!"

Michael appraised me calmly. He was drinking from a teacup, and he rested his eyes on me over its rim.

"What's happening at dinner?"

"I'm taking you and Lucy and Diana out to dinner in Penley," I said. This had not occurred to me before I said it, but once I had said it it sounded like the best idea possible.

"What's the occasion?"

"Must there be an occasion?"

"Is Abel invited?" the doctor said.

"Abel," I announced, trembling slightly with fear and excitement, "is gone."

Though no longer drinking, the doctor continued to hold his teacup in front of his mouth as he watched me. He looked at me over the rim of the cup for a full minute or two before he spoke again.

"You took him to the orphanage?" he said at last.

Now I paused for a full minute. Then I said this:

"What else could I mean?"

The doctor watched me over his teacup for another minute, and then he lowered the cup so that he could stare at the ground. I did not move. Finally the doctor came to some understanding with himself, and he looked me firmly in the eye. "Which train would you like to get?" he said.

"The six o'clock," I answered.

The doctor turned around and began walking back to his house.

"I'll go ask Lucy," he said.

I almost leaped in the air as I ran to Diana's house. I began knocking as soon as my fist could reach the door and I did not stop until it opened.

Diana was wearing a long white nightgown and rubbing her eyes. I rushed forward to take her hot sleepy body in my arms, and I walked with her inside far enough to shut the door behind me.

"Diana," I said, and I kissed her. Not yet fully awake, she neither kissed me back nor resisted. "Can you come out to dinner with us tonight?"

"With who?" she said. "What did you do?"

"I sent the boy away," I said.

"Where?" she said, pulling out of my arms. "For how long?"

"Forever," I said. "It's all taken care of. Don't worry, Diana."

She relaxed back into my arms and looked up at me smiling, and I remarked to myself that I loved her.

"Who's coming to dinner?"

"A perfect foursome," I answered. "You, and me, and Dr. Michael A. Ericsson, and Mrs. Lucy J. Ericsson."

My delight was contagious and Diana laughed.

"Will we be playing bridge?" she said.

"Bridge," I said, as I took her hand and spun her around, "pinochle, poker, spades, hearts, and Chinese *ding pai.*"

Diana laughed again and life seemed altogether easy.

"*Ding pai?*"

"*Ding pai,* my love," I said, "is a simple game. I will meet you at the station for the six o'clock train."

"The train station?"

"We are going," I said, "to the restaurant in Penley." I turned around and began to walk away; Diana stood in her doorway; I spun around and called out to her. "The *nice* restaurant in Penley!"

I walked back to the green house with my face flushed and my heart dancing. There were many hours to pass before it was time for dinner; I would even have to eat a meal or two before then; I felt annoyed at having to find some purpose for myself, but the annoyance turned to exhilaration at the sheer abundance and wastefulness of time.

Upstairs I walked toward my study with the intention of

taking out my microscope, but I stopped at Abel's door, half surprised to see it. I suppose that I expected it to be gone. I remembered that I would have to pack away his things, and I stepped over the threshold sincerely intending to do this, so that it would be done before dinner and I could return to a clean and empty house.

But I stood in the boy's room looking at his purple shirt tangled across his desk chair and the pile of books on the foot of the bed for only a few seconds before I stepped quickly out again. There was still a lock on the door, I told myself, and I did not need the space—why waste my time cleaning? I began to panic briefly when I could not find the padlock, but then I remembered where it was, in a desk drawer.

Once I had locked Abel's door I left my house again and went to the store. I had the feeling, though I knew it was unlikely, that Gabriel the shopkeeper had spoken to Michael already. He did not ask me where Abel was, why I was dressed up, or why I wanted to hang around the store for the first time in many months. He merely looked at me when I came in and offered me a cup of tea. Eventually a few other old men came in, and I had a grand time with them eating sandwiches and playing checkers.

It was clear from Lucy's lovely dress and her cheerful countenance that she knew nothing about the occasion for dinner to make her feel anything but mildly excited at an excuse to dress up. She and Diana exchanged compliments and felt Lucy's belly while the doctor stared thoughtfully into the forest. I bounced up the steps to the platform and said good evening.

"Hello, Joseph," the doctor said. "How are you?"

"Brilliant," I said, and that was the end of that conversation. I greeted Lucy and she greeted me; I kissed Diana and she kissed me.

"What is the occasion for dinner, Joseph?" asked the doctor's wife.

I glanced my eyes at the doctor, but Diana spoke first. "He's a carefree bachelor again," she said.

"His orphan Abel has been sent away," Michael said. "As was inevitable," he added, seeing that Lucy did not understand why this was occasion for a party. "We are celebrating a job well done."

"Oh," she said. "Well then, Joseph, congratulations, I guess. Good riddance!"

"Thank you," I said.

Lucy shook my hand vigorously, making her husband and Diana laugh.

Diana, although dressed formally, looked younger than I remember her ever looking before. Her eyes were bright. We held hands as the train pulled in and I removed mine only to pay for the tickets.

"Four to Penley," I said, waving away the doctor's money without turning around. We sat, the four of us, in facing seats, and we had a very interesting conversation. It was essentially a conspiracy made up of me and the doctor for the purpose of entertaining Lucy, who knew very little about Abel's stay in Bettley, and of distracting Diana from alluding to anything.

During a lull the doctor brought up the subject of painting. "I haven't heard you mention Mondrian for a long time," he said to me. This was not the sort of remark that the man would make naturally, although Lucy did not seem to notice this. Perhaps she did but assumed—as she had no reason not to—that her husband was merely taking responsibility for the smoothness of the conversation. Perhaps it even struck her as evidence of his concern for her amusement. In any case the remark could not have struck my ear more like a coded signal if he had tapped it out in Morse.

"I haven't thought about him for a long time," I said. "No, that isn't true—I recently realized something."

Lucy asked me what my special interest in Mondrian was, and at the doctor's prompting, I recounted my visit to the retrospective to her and to Diana, who knew about it only vaguely. Lucy asked whether it was Mondrian's skill that had upset me, and I explained that it was not.

"The point," I said, "is not even that they're beautiful. I think they are, but it doesn't matter—the point is that they are painting reduced to its very essence. Vertical, horizontal, black, white, and three colors. Everything that came before it was leading up to it, and it made anything else after it seem completely gratuitous, even actively wasteful."

I prepared to go on and explain a recent revelation: that really zero may imply the numbers but they still need to be said, that the ground does not make buildings moot, that even Cartesian graphs and primary colors could be presented in an infinite number of ways. But Diana spoke and caught me completely off guard.

"But, Joseph," she said, "that's like making a chemical analysis of love."

"I'm sorry," I said, "what?"

"It's like reducing the state of being in love to a chemical analysis of pheromones. Pheromones aren't the meaning of love, they're the means. All Mondrian did was paint the tools of painting."

"That's brilliant," I said.

The doctor agreed and added, "He wasn't doing anything but tacking paintbrushes to the wall."

"Anyone could have done it," Lucy said.

"Anyway, Joe," Diana said, "he did what he did and now it's done, but it doesn't have anything to do with you. You can't paint Mondrian's paintings and he couldn't paint yours."

This last sentence that she spoke affected me as Mondrian's windmill once had; I grabbed Diana's arm with one hand and the arm of my seat with the other.

"Will you say that one more time?"

"I said that Mondrian couldn't paint your paintings any more than you could paint his."

Lucy and Diana smiled at each other and the doctor smiled at me as I gaped at all of them. Finally, after what seemed like several seconds, I released Diana's arm.

"Thank you," I said.

Our dinner in Penley was wonderful.

CHAPTER ELEVEN

I implied earlier in this story that I never went into a museum again after the Mondrian retrospective, but in fact I spent all my time in the picture galleries for the several months it took me to develop a new personality. In that time I saw very many paintings of the angel Michael serenely piercing a writhing devil in the eye with a lance. I never failed to be revolted by the angel's serenity. How could he act so pitilessly? The answer had to be that he knew that his action was just—that he was good.

I have described already Michael's treatment of Abel after I had beaten the boy into a daze: he was as gentle with him as he would be with a baby. I have not yet described, simply because it did not fit anywhere, a conversation that he and I had about the incident later:

"I don't give a damn about the little bastard, Joseph,"

Michael had said to me. "I only care about the way he is making you behave."

At the time that he said this I was in no position to give it much thought, but when some months afterwards it came to mind I spent two or three days trying to reconcile for myself what seemed to be my friend's inconsistency. I quickly realized that I had been no less inconsistent, but in the opposite way: I felt physically ill whenever I thought of Abel's pain and loneliness, but I also beat him, screamed at him, and jailed him in his room. The doctor, meanwhile, while totally without sympathy, could not have treated Abel with better sense or more good humor. And the difference between us was simple: the doctor always acted dispassionately, but I was distracted by my pity. Therefore it is not enough, I think, to say that the angel Michael can be pitiless because he is good—he can only be good because he is pitiless.

But the angel's triumph does not merely lead to the devil's suffering, it does not cause it incidentally: it requires it. It could not exist without it, any more than the suffering could exist without the triumph. And in what sense is he good that must have evil? For what crime, too, does Michael punish the devil, or to prevent what crime does he stab him? Perhaps the devil, given the chance, would do the same thing to him. Then what difference is there between them? There is no piercer or pierced, it seems to me, but only a piercing.

Or if there is a difference, it is in their points of view. The angel Michael looking down knows that he is good and that his actions must therefore be good, that they are necessary in themselves and necessary to the world, and not to be regretted. Even his lance's victim and his suffering are part of the good, for all the painting rests on the lance, and the painting is beautiful. All flowers grow up out of dirt. But the devil looks up knowing that he is low and evil and so is his death, and so is the angel that murders him.

CHAPTER TWELVE

Some time later, when the Ericssons had just bought a house in the city, I took them and Diana to dinner again. After eating in Penley we rode the train back north, sitting quietly and watching the night through the windows as Lucy nursed her son. I took Diana's hand and excused us from the company. I led her through the cars to the end of the train where there was a small uncovered deck. We stood there together in the cool, clear night, huddled together on the sooty deck, watching and watched by the flashing trees, and I asked Diana to marry me, and much to my luck she said yes.

We agreed without speaking to stretch out and enjoy the moment as long as possible, and we stood in the clacking wind until we started to feel the chill. Then we rushed back inside laughing and hurried to tell Michael and Lucy what we had decided. Diana was flushed and I was lightheaded; we stood expectantly holding hands. Michael looked up from his baby and saw our expressions and stopped talking, and he and Lucy waited for us to tell.

"Joseph just asked me to marry him!" Diana said.

There was a pause.

"What did you say?" Lucy asked.

"Oh," Diana said laughing, "I said yes!"

Lucy jumped up to congratulate her, leaving her son to his father's arms, and they embraced, and as they stood sharing connubial secrets I sat down in Lucy's seat.

The doctor calmly shook my hand. "Spur of the moment?" he asked.

"No," I said, "I've been waiting for a long time."

Diana heard this and turned for a moment from Lucille to punch me on the shoulder. "No kidding, Joseph," she said, "you move like a turtle."

I touched her hand and she turned back.

"Congratulations, Joe," the doctor said, warmly now, and he shook my hand again. The Ericssons insisted, although it was late and we had eaten dessert in Penley, that we come over for coffee and cake to celebrate. We sat in their dining room with the windows open, and the sheer joy of sitting with Diana and our friends on a clear night eating cake was so great in me that I thought my heart would burst. That night I slept at Diana's, and the next morning, while Diana was at the doctor's office, I began moving my things out of the green house.

Only that morning did Diana tell me what she had hidden from me until then, that she had been brought to Bettley, and therefore also to me, by the same disease that had killed my parents. She had refused when diagnosed to be sent to a sanitarium, and so her doctor had suggested that she move to her family's old house in Bettley, where the air would be good for her lungs and the quiet would force her to rest. Her symptoms had largely passed even before I arrived, but she had had no pressing reason to leave again—now, engaged to be married, she did. After a quick breakfast, therefore, she hurried to Michael's office to get herself a clean bill of health. After a brief examination he gave it.

The afternoon we spent together, warmly clothed and walking north on the road as far as New Salem and back. We were making a point of spending the day together because we knew that we would be busy for the next several months. Diana wanted to organize our wedding as quickly as possible, and I was learning to paint. The second morning of our engagement we rode the train together to Penley; after we had agreed on a return train, Diana went off to see printers and florists and caterers and I went off to buy newsprint and charcoal.

After six months Diana had assembled her childhood dream of a wedding, and I had taught myself how to draw well enough to really begin learning. I was surprised to discover that I had ideas, and more than ideas, artistic inspirations. At first it was only strong convictions about ways of doing things: I tended to draw schematically, for example, and very emotionally, and I had to force myself to pay attention to draftsmanship. But as soon as I had gotten some sense of how to make marks on paper I began to have sudden inspirations—I would sometimes wake up in the middle of the night with a figure or a color in my mind that would not leave me until I had expressed it on paper.

We had a wonderful time at the wedding. Diana was very happy, and I was delighted in many ways in addition to my great delight in her. Not least I got to know Diana's parents and was thrilled to discover that I liked them much better than I had ever liked my own, and that they seemed to like me. I also learned at the reception that my sober friend Michael can drink me under the table, and once I had drunk enough I learned how to dance. We even had a yellow layer cake with coconut filling, white icing, and pink flowers.

After the wedding we returned north, but we knew that it would not be for long. I finished shutting up the green house quickly—there was little in it that I needed. I took my clothing and one or two books as souvenirs. (I had completely lost my interest in disease, and it never came back—I have long since lost track even of those one or two souvenirs.) Diana did not want her children to grow up in a town without a theater or a bookstore. At the same time, the doctor and his wife were now settled in the city, and Bettley without our friends would be still more lonely.

Before we left the town I left Diana at home one morning and took a walk in the pine forest with my metal shovel. Since taking my last walk with Abel I had maintained a distant relationship with the trees: I looked at them respectfully from my window and they looked back. When I felt inclined to take a walk I walked on the road. I do not mean to say that I was scared; certainly I felt terrible regret sometimes and I did not like to think about what I had done; but for the most part I simply felt that I had completed, for good or ill, whatever I had been meant to do with the trees. But before we left I wanted to mark Abel's grave. I could hardly carry a tombstone with me, even if I could have gotten one, and so for a memorial I planned to drive my metal shovel into the earth.

It was in the early spring and the day was beautiful: the air was fresh and alive and the sun tall and youthful. I carried the shovel over my shoulder and walked with a light heart. The fact that I would soon be leaving the forest made me feel free, it made the day like an unexpected gift. I enjoyed the walk so much that I think I walked too far. Perhaps I simply did not walk in quite the right direction; in any case, I never found the elm tree. As the afternoon grew later I began to worry about Diana, and to worry about Diana worrying about me, and finally I decided that a strange single elm tree in a forest of pines was a better monument to Abel than anything I could do. I walked into New Salem and rode the train home. Later, when Diana was pregnant with our second child and we were discussing names, I suggested that if it were a boy we might want to name it Abel. Diana replied to this by reminding me that in the Jewish tradition it is not done to name a child after a living person, and I left it at that; in the event we had a second daughter.